BECOMING MOON

Craig A. Hart

This book is a work of fiction. Names, characters, places, and incidents either are products of the author's imagination or are used fictitiously. Any resemblance to actual events or locales or persons, living or dead, is entirely coincidental.

Copyright © 2015 by Craig A. Hart

All rights reserved, including the right of reproduction in whole or in part.

Front cover by Amygdala Design

ISBN-13: 978-1512234121
ISBN-10: 1512234125

To Andrew and Christopher
May you always live in a world of choices.

*There is a time when each man
is faced with the test of his existence.*
— *Nigel Moon*

Part One

I met him during one of the self-indulgent sojourns north. I had become fond of these pilgrimages, the ones in search of my prodigal muse, having convinced myself they were an essential part of the creative process. There was something about writing in the same place every day that turned task to chore. It stunted the imagination. It dampened the enthusiasm. It blunted the honed edge of my prose. I found repetition distracting and, in the throes of boredom, became a master of avoidance. At those times I was much better at *not* writing, becoming intensely productive in all things unrelated. My apartment was never cleaner, nor my bookshelves so organized, nor my e-mail inbox so empty than when not writing. But ennui would descend and there was nothing for it but to pack up the tools of my trade, gas up the car, and point north. It was good for writing, but in truth, I liked to travel and Michigan's Upper Peninsula often put me in the writing mood. The fragrance of summer, the unbearable whimsy of fall, the crushing eternity of winter, and, finally, the sanctification of spring: all served to stoke the creative fire.

When I headed north, this time at the end of October, full of good intentions to finish the aging novel living on my computer's hard drive, snow had begun to fall. Little specks floated down, hit the windshield, and were whisked out of sight over the car roof. It was already dark. The snowflakes flashed through the headlight beams as I drove up 131 out of Grand Rapids. I turned on the radio, but the noise was grating. I turned it off almost immediately.

A ding and a red light indicated low fuel. I had forgotten an important step in my ritual. I glanced in the backseat to check for my duffel bag. It sat there, silent, and I breathed a little easier. I could be a creature of habit, not in all things, but when it came to writing there were elements of the superstitious. Over the last few years, the northern sojourns had taken on a spiritual quality, to the point that I was afraid—and I do not use the word lightly—to vary. Forgetting to top off the tank was a major misstep in the process and caused a stab of dread.

The previous exit sign had advertised gasoline and the off ramp was coming up quickly. I was already halfway past and had to drive over the median to make it. I heard a loud honk from the rear and saw a black SUV, its headlights beaming directly into my rearview mirror. I flipped the mirror up to dull the glare. The SUV pulled so close, its grill almost disappeared from my view. I could just make out the driver: a youngish male wearing a baseball hat with the bill ironed flat. He was gesturing with his right hand and steering with his left.

The gas stations were to the left off the ramp. I hoped the SUV was going the other way. I was in the wrong and in no mood for confrontation. I signaled left and the other driver followed suit. I saw lights ahead and made the turn. If I could get inside the station, perhaps the presence of others would keep the situation from escalating.

The snow had increased and now affected visibility, but I saw the station ahead. Then I pulled nearer and saw it was not a station at all. It was a church, small with wooden siding, standing white against the darkness of the horizon and seeming to absorb the falling snow. In front of the church stood two sets of three crosses. The crosses had hoses and handles, and people were pumping gas onto the ground. The church windows were alive with light. The front door stood open and through the opening I saw pews full of people. They stood and appeared to be singing.

I drove into the lot, parked, and stepped out of the car. The black SUV pulled in behind me. The driver's door opened and the man stepped out. He still wore the flat brimmed hat, but now I noticed horns protruding from the sides of his head. The hat balanced between them. His eyes flashed and his mouth moved, but I could not hear what he was saying over the sound of the singing from the church.

Oh! precious is the flow
That makes me white as snow—

The snow had picked up even more, stinging my face and driving against the outside of my car with sounds like spitting snakes. The man from the SUV walked toward me and his eyes were red. He opened his mouth and a forked tongue rolled out and quivered at me. His hand went to his pocket and I knew he had a gun. I felt something wet on my shoe. The gasoline pumped from the crosses pooled around my feet. The gas changed color. It stained the ground where the snow was beginning to stick and turned the flakes blood red.

No other fount I know,
Nothing but the blood of Jesus.

I ran, stumbling, for the church. I felt the man behind me, and I think I screamed. I fell through the door, landing on my face.

The singing stopped. I felt everyone turn to look at me. I pushed myself to my hands and knees. The tile beneath my hands was cold and the room was quiet. I looked up. An Indian man stood behind the counter, a phone in his hand.

"Sir," he asked, "you want me to call the police?"

I looked around. The pews were gone, replaced by aisles of snack food, fuel tank additives, and road maps. The people were there, but they were not dressed in church clothes and certainly were not singing. They looked down at me with a mixture of fear, curiosity, and pity. I got to my feet, slowly and warily, and remembered the man from the SUV. I turned and saw him standing in the doorway, holding the door open, looking at me with the same confused expression as the others. His hat was still there, but the horns had disappeared. He looked entirely normal, even more scared than I was. His hand came out of his pocket and he held a cell phone. I turned and ran from the station. As I pushed past the SUV driver, I heard him say to the Indian clerk, "He be trippin'."

I sat in my car and gripped the steering wheel. My whole body shook. I clenched my jaw to keep my teeth from chattering. I looked around the parking lot. The church was gone, the crosses were gone, the blood . . . all of it gone. In its place was a perfectly normal Shell gas station, now full of people who thought they had just witnessed the meltdown of a severely unstable person. I gripped the steering wheel and brought my forehead down against it, first lightly and then harder. It hurt, but I was happy to feel something.

I coasted into the next station, running on fumes, and got gas without incident. I kept an eye on the rearview mirror for the next fifty miles, half expecting to see a police cruiser behind me. But the snow had increased and was now a full-fledged snowstorm. If the police had been called, which was unlikely, they were doubtless too busy with road concerns to track me down. The weather report had said nothing of this. Thirty percent chance of snow flurries, it had said. Visibility continually decreased and was down to a mere two car lengths. The road was mostly deserted; every now and then I came upon the vehicle of a more cautious, sensible driver moving slowly, hazard lights blinking. I considered finding lodging for the night as the snow continued to fall and increase, but the thought of the added expense changed my mind.

It was 8:30 p.m. when I drove into St. Francis. Founded in the late 1600s by French explorers, the town enjoyed a period of significance during the height of the fur trade. It then diminished in relevance as the demand for New World fur products decreased, but was now important to me as the first planned stop of my trip.

The Jesuit was a bar on the edge of the tiny downtown district. It was one of the oldest buildings in town. The site first hosted a log trading post and then a warehouse that burned down in the early 1800s. This was replaced with a stone structure that served as warehouse turned dancehall turned general store. In the mid-1900s it served as apartments but became vacant after the bank foreclosed. It stood empty until 1982 when the current owner bought, renovated, and opened the bar that now occupied a vital place in my ritual: my first drink in the Upper Peninsula.

The Jesuit was only half-full. The snow had kept some at home and driven others to the bar. I looked into the familiar, dim corner booth. There was a young couple seated there. They huddled over some manner of fruity martini, making lovers' faces at one another. I wondered if they were old enough to drink and asked them so.

The young man looked up, still flushed from his conquest. "Excuse me?"

"I asked if you two were old enough to be drinking. What are you, eighteen? Nineteen?"

"I'm twenty-one." His voice held the contempt and arrogance of one too immature to know what they do not know.

"I need this booth."

They both looked at me as if I had threatened to cook and eat them.

"We're not moving," he said.

"I need the booth."

"It's not busy in here. There are several other booths."

"I always sit at this one."

"I've never seen you here before."

"Not surprising, considering you have only been drinking for, what, a week?" I pointed to the martini. "What is that, fruit punch?"

"Look, shithead, we were here first. Stop bothering us."

"This is my regular booth."

"Get the hell away from us or I'll kick your ass!"

We were beginning to make a scene. The young man half rose from the booth and his face said he was not bluffing. I performed a mental check on my combat readiness. The past ten years had not been kind to my physical state. Writing was taxing in many ways, but not as an effective cardio regimen. The bit of flab around my middle could attest to that. I was about twenty pounds overweight with a depressing amount of muscle mass. The kid was not exactly ready for the boxing circuit, but he certainly looked in better shape than I felt. I was relieved when a familiar hand fell on my shoulder.

"Is there a problem here?"

"Yeah," the kid said, "this asshole's trying to take our booth."

"He's a regular," the newcomer said. He was around sixty and the hair missing from his head reappeared over his lip in the form of a robust, unapologetic moustache. He smiled at the kid. "Go ahead and choose another table, son. Your drinks are on the house tonight."

They hesitated, but the promise of free drinks—and the barman's friendly but unwavering face—persuaded them.

I slid onto the worn faux leather of the booth seat. It felt like coming home. "Thanks for your help, Archer."

"Good to see ya," he said. "Picked a bad night for it, though. How was the bridge?"

"I took it slow."

"Your usual?"

I nodded. He left to make the drink and I looked around the bar. I saw a few people I recognized, but I did not usually pay much attention to faces. Instead I listened to conversations and noticed mannerisms, tics, and habits. It was a common complaint of those I dated: "You never see me. You look right through me. And then you comment on how I hold my fork. How can you be so observant and yet not notice I exist?" They never understood the writer's psyche. Then again, neither did I. No one did.

There was one person who caught my attention: an older man sitting in the corner booth directly across from mine. He wore a red plaid hunting cap. His face was grizzled and almost as worn as his brown corduroy jacket. Gray hair showed beneath the cap. He held a book in his hands and stared at the pages intently. I squinted, trying to make out the title in the dim light of the bar, but my prescription was outdated by a few years.

There was a dull clunk and where my table had been empty now sat a Johnnie Walker Black with Perrier. There were cheaper drinks, but I knew what I liked. And this was what I liked at the Jesuit.

"Who is the old guy with the paperback?"

Archer did not even look over. "You don't recognize him? That's Nigel Moon."

"The writer?"

"Very same. Fella's had a bestselling book in each of the last five years."

"What is he doing here?"

"He's from this general area originally. He passes through every now and then, but he's been in pretty regular the last couple of weeks."

"Is he friendly? I mean, how would he react if I introduced myself?"

Archer preened his moustache. "He's a strange fella. Friendly enough, but doesn't like lots of questions."

I took a drink. "Neither do I."

Nigel Moon did not look up as I approached and continued reading even after I stood next to his booth. He did, however, speak.

"Don't stand over me, boy. Makes me twitchy."

"I understand you are Nigel Moon. The writer."

"That's what they tell me."

"I also do a little writing."

Moon put down the tattered paperback and his lined faced wrinkled further. He pushed back the cap, revealing deep eyes lurking beneath brows in dire need of a trim. The eyes flashed. "What did you say your name was?"

I told him.

"Can't say I know it. Been published?"

"A few times."

"Books, short stories, technical manuals, ad copy?"

"Two novels and a handful of shorts."

"You look pretty young. How old are you?"

"Pushing forty."

"I'm pulling seventy, so that's pretty young. How long you been writing?

"Going on twenty years."

"You've survived on two novels in twenty years?"

"The first was something of a hit. I still receive some royalties from it. Otherwise, I rely on extreme frugality."

"So writing is your only gig."

"It is now."

"I can respect that. Doesn't seem prudent. But if you acted sensibly you wouldn't be a real writer at all, now would you?"

Although it was not part of my regular routine, I felt an unexpected desire to sit and talk with this man. Perhaps it was simply because he was a writer, one who had lived the life and seen it all. There was a certain magnetism about him, a charisma that drew me. I hesitated, then said, "Would you mind if I joined you?"

"I suppose not. Just don't act like you're having a good time. I have the reputation of being an ill-tempered hermit. I'd like to maintain that image. It keeps the riffraff at bay."

"Are you?"

"Am I what?"

"An ill-tempered hermit."

"Depends on the company and how many fool questions they ask." He picked up the book and made a good show of reading a few lines. He turned the page and looked up at me. "So what do you want?"

"I wanted to meet you. One writer drawn to another, I suppose."

"Ah. The gravity of the creative. I do remember that from my younger days. Seeking out other writers, especially older writers, hoping their experience would rub off on me."

"And did it?"

"Who can say? If so, it took some time. I didn't start seeing any success until late in the game. Sounds like you hit it early."

"In my twenties."

"Times have been lean since?"

"Quite."

"Ever thought about getting a day job?"

"Every day."

"And?"

"It would seem like something of a setback."

Moon chuckled and it seemed at least a few of the facial wrinkles were laugh lines. "That's the story of life, boy. Especially the life of an artist. You're lucky you had a position to be set back from. Most don't even get that far."

"That does not make it any easier."

"Gotta meet expenses. The life of a starving artist is only romantic on the big screen or the printed page. I lived it and quickly discovered I didn't enjoy suffering for my art. Didn't mean I loved it less; just that I was more materialistic than I thought. What're you drinking?"

"Johnnie Walker Black."

"Good choice. Maybe a little too good."

"Maybe I like a few comforts. And there are more expensive drinks."

"I drank a lot of Pabst."

"Okay, so you are the more legitimate artist."

Moon sat back a little and raised his hands in mock surrender. "Relax, boy. This isn't a contest."

"Do you always judge other people's drink choices?"

"Always. You can tell a lot about a person by what they drink."

"And what does my choice say about me?"

"Either you're living in the past or trying the whole 'fake it until you make it' bullshit. As you say, there are more expensive drinks, so I don't think it's the latter. And besides, your clothes are shit. So I'd guess the former."

"And what are you drinking?"

Moon gave me the rueful smile of someone beaten at his own game. "Pabst."

"Living in the past?"

"I developed a taste for it."

"Maybe we are not too different."

"Most writers aren't. We're a strange breed. I don't trust naturally happy, well-adjusted writers. I've never met an artist enamored with life. I don't think the two can coexist. You read my stuff?"

I took a double drink. "No, although I have heard about it. Sorry."

"It was pathetic to ask."

There was a moment of awkward silence before I ventured, "Are you working on anything new? The bartender says you had five bestsellers in as many years."

"It was a good stretch. Didn't come free, though." He looked as if he wanted to continue, so I waited as he drank and read a few lines from the book. At last he turned a page and looked up. "Art can turn into business without the artist noticing. That's the real tragedy."

"Is that what happened to you?"

"What did I tell you about asking fool questions?"

"Sorry."

He finished off his Pabst. "Success came late. I'd resigned myself to being a hack forever." He closed the book and pushed it aside. "Not that going unpublished makes you a hack, by the way. That's just how I felt. Truth be told, I don't trust the publishing racket any more than I trust happy artists. Goddamn gatekeepers. Censorship in angel's wings." He raised his empty glass toward Archer, who nodded. "When the contract came along, I jumped at it. The book was well received, a critical success with a tidy profit. The publisher pushed for another book, hoping to capitalize on the public's interest before I became old news. I stalled as long as I could, but the money dried up and by then I'd gotten used to paying bills on time. The publisher knew my position and played hardball. Before I knew it, I'd signed a contract extension for six more books."

"Six books?"

"It's a lot, I know. But my star was finally rising. I was flush with success. I saw the figure in the contract and convinced myself I could do it."

"Your publisher placed a lot of faith in you. They were on the hook for six publications just as much as you were."

"Not really. There was a clause in the contract that allowed the contract to expire based on sales numbers. If one book failed to meet projections, they were off the hook."

"Bastards."

"Artists tend to be crap at business. Even so, I threw myself into the task at hand. Each book became more difficult. After book three, I began sincerely hoping they would fail. But the damn things kept selling. By then I had made a name for myself and, along with it, an obnoxiously faithful following."

"Must be awful."

"I know it sounds ungrateful. But I was running dry. It wasn't about the art anymore. It was all business. I began to dread writing, then to hate it. I even considered writing a deliberately shoddy book to drive down sales but still had too much artistic pride to actually do it."

A fresh Pabst arrived and Moon drank half before continuing.

"I slogged through book four. It sold. I drank my way through book five. Damn thing sold."

"And book six?"

"Not written yet. Not so much as a single word."

"Any ideas?"

"None. My typewriter is closed in a box. I can't even stand the sight of it. I'm out of paper, but haven't purchased any in months. My art has become my nemesis. Because of the goddamn dollar." He drained the beer.

"You use a typewriter?"

"Old habits."

"So what are you going to do?"

"I have no idea," he said. "I have no fucking idea. It's got to be written or I'm in breach of contract. I've written literally millions of words over the years. You'd think one book would be doable. But I'm tapped out. I'm an artist who's come to hate his art. I used to think that finding too much success early, as you did, would be a bad thing. But peaking late may be worse."

I squirmed at the insinuation I had peaked early. It certainly did not raise my hopes I would be able to make a comeback. The ice had melted in my drink, watering it down well beyond a smoothing dilution. I drank it anyway. I could not afford to waste it.

"I can tell you one thing," he said. "No matter how it turns out, this will be my last book. I'm just too damn tired. Burned out." The lines on his face deepened. I had never seen a sadder person and I saw the laugh lines were not actually laugh lines at all. He brought the palm of his hand down on the table. Both glasses jumped. I jumped with them. "But it ends here," he said. "This year. This winter. I've decided to make St. Francis my Waterloo, my Maginot Line, my Custer's Last Stand."

The look in his eyes told me I did not have to tell him the history behind the examples. I knew they were purposely chosen.

"That seems somewhat dramatic," I said. "It will come to you. And if it does not, the only one hurt will be your publisher, for whom you have already expressed a good deal of disdain."

"And now I feel as if you haven't heard a word I've said. It's here my lifelong love affair with writing will come down to a single crushing defeat. It's not about the publisher or even my readers. It is, quite selfishly, about myself. You're still young. I'm in my twilight years, and I look back to see a life spent pursuing a single purpose. To come to the end and be unable to do the one thing that has made everything worthwhile . . . do you know why Hemingway shot himself?"

"He was depressed."

"He was unable to write. This giant, revered and worshipped for his contributions to literature, could no longer compose a comprehensible sentence. I'm not comparing myself to Hemingway. I'm just saying I know how he must've felt."

I looked into his eyes and they were wintery, cold, devoid of hope, and for a moment I thought I was looking into Hemingway's eyes. They were brown and set into a broad face weathered by time and circumstance. Perhaps it was no coincidence Moon had come to the Upper Peninsula, much loved by Hemingway, to tackle his life's greatest challenge. At least he had not chosen Sun Valley.

Moon edged out of the booth. "Hell, I'm tired. I haven't talked so much since my last pretentious interview on NPR. Staying in town?"

"No. Leaving tomorrow."

"Well, then it was good meeting you. Always nice to see a writer still pursuing the dream." He reached for the ragged paperback and I finally saw the title: *The Lonely Peninsula: A Novel*. The book's author was Nigel Moon.

* * *

The growing storm did not let up. By morning a sleepy St. Francis awoke to find itself beneath a thick quilt of snow, with more on the way. The state police issued a warning to travelers, requesting they stay off the road except in extreme emergencies. The schools closed and by midmorning the most coveted sledding destinations were awash in children, with a few intrepid parents standing out amid the herd.

This was the morning I would continue the journey to my rented cabin. By the schedule, I would arrive, get settled in, enjoy my first drink at the site of my new lodgings, and spend the evening reading one of the books designed to prime the pump of creativity. The morning after, I would begin writing. Or, at least, begin the attempts at writing.

Perhaps it was the growing difficulty I had experienced with the current novel. Perhaps it was the warning from the state police regarding their lengthy response times in the event of an accident. Perhaps it was the feeling of nostalgia I got when looking out my room window at the snow covered streets of St. Francis, a town that reminded me a great deal of the one I grew up in. Or perhaps it was the meeting with Nigel Moon the night before. The talk had impacted me deeply in a way I could not fully understand, but there had been a connection I had not experienced with another human being for many years. It was a feeling strong enough that I was aware of its existence. While this may not be much of an indication for most, it was striking for me as I had never had much insight into my own emotional state. And the experiences that elicited a noticeable mood shift, other than a negative one, were noteworthy. It may have been that. But whatever it was caused me to make this new departure from ritual and I decided to delay my trip across the Peninsula for at least a day.

I left the hotel and got into my car. I turned the key and was rewarded with a sickening click. The battery was dead. I tried several more times without so much as a whine from the engine. I placed a call to the local tow shop.

"Yeah, we can help you," the man said, "but you're gonna have to wait awhile. We're swamped with this snowstorm. You'd think people up here would know how to drive, but so help me if they don't forget every single year."

"How long?"

"Gimme your number and I'll call you. It'll be a while."

I swore enough to attract attention, but soon accepted the hopelessness of the situation and went next door for a cup of coffee. The Java Hut was busy. People, who never seem to tire of discussing the weather, sat around making their predictions about what heavy snowfall in October meant for the remainder of the season.

"I remember back in '91," one older man said, "we had dis same type o' storm on, I believe, dis very same date. And that year we had snow t'all the way tah June."

"That wasn't '91," his wife corrected with a roll of her eyes that suggested she had never seen a man so ignorant. "It was '95. I remember because that was the year of your first heart attack."

"Oh, dat's right," the man said. "I remember now. Ninety-one 'twas da year we had dat big windstorm in September. Blew down da back shed, as I recall."

I ordered a black coffee.

"Do you know if the library is open today?" I asked the barista.

"I doubt it," she said. "My kids are home from school and the library usually closes when the schools close. Frustrating, because I'd love to send them over there on snow days."

I moved off toward the window. I knew there was a bookstore about a mile down the road. But I would also have to walk, so I finished my coffee while it was hot and let it warm my insides before I walked out into the snow.

The walk was not as bad as anticipated. The temperature was relatively mild, not the biting chill of deep winter. I arrived at the Book Den just as my lungs began to labor. The bookstore was a single room, warm and pleasant. From two speakers above the counter came the sound of a Brahms concerto. There was a decent used book section and from there wafted the intoxicating mustiness of old pages.

I found my way to the local authors section. There, prominently displayed, were the last five books by Nigel Moon, all in shiny dust jackets. I began thumbing through them, beginning with the first and making my way to the most recent. Even reading select passages, I could see the writer's craft disintegrating with each successive book. The first was well written enough, even masterful at times, with little turns of phrase and pieces of lyricism that were nothing short of poetic. But as the books continued, the lyricism descended into declaration, the poetry into forced sentences that struggled to convey their most basic meaning. By the final book, I was stunned at the transformation. It could not be the same author. The artistry was gone. There was no heart. It was an academic exercise without the intellectual insight. I felt embarrassed as I read the last couple of pages and then slid the books back onto the shelf. I searched the rest of the section, but did not see the title Moon had been reading in the bar.

I inquired at the counter.

"I think we have one copy of it," the blurry-eyed young man with dreads monotoned. He was trying very hard to convey a complete lack of interest in anything and was succeeding admirably. He pointed in the general direction of the used book section. "You could check back there."

"Just . . . check back there? You are not sure of your own inventory?"

"We don't see that many."

"But you think you have one."

"If we have one, it would be in the used book section. Seems like someone traded one in not long ago, but I don't remember where I stocked it exactly. We don't see that many."

"Rare, are they?"

"I don't know, man."

"You just said as much."

"I said we don't see that many. Doesn't mean they're, like, rare."

An unexpected feeling of hatred welled up inside me, hatred for this greasy hippy and his marijuana-induced lack of customer service. I paused for a moment so I could fully enjoy the sensation. And then I turned on my heel and walked back to the used book section. To my surprise, the books were well organized by author's last name, a task no doubt performed by the clerk during a rare sober afternoon. I plucked the single copy of *The Lonely Peninsula* from between Montgomery's *Anne of Green Gables* and *Beloved* by Toni Morrison. It was the same paperback edition Moon had been reading, although in slightly better condition.

I slipped the book into the inside pocket of my coat and headed for the exit. I expected a challenge from the clerk, but I should not have worried. He was too busy sitting on a stool behind the counter with his head tilted back, counting the holes in the fiberboard ceiling tiles.

* * *

I considered going back to my room. Retreating under the covers with an endless supply of coffee and this mysterious book was appealing, but the thought of being alone gave me pause. It was a strange reaction, being alone typically a state I actively pursued and vigorously defended. But today, perhaps because of the inherent loneliness of snowfall, I felt the need to be, if not in contact with people, at least in close proximity to them.

The Jesuit was not far and the comforting feeling that washed over me upon entering seemed to confirm the decision, as did Archer's warm welcome. I was the only customer at the moment. They would come.

"Back again?" Archer said. "I thought you'd have left town by now."

"I decided to wait at least another day. My car would not start this morning. The snow and all."

"I'm surprised you didn't hire some sled dogs."

Talk of abandoning the ritual made me uncomfortable, as if discussion would make it a more serious transgression. "Any sign of Nigel Moon?"

"He doesn't usually come in before one or two in the afternoon." He glanced at the clock. "You're at it early for a snow day."

"I tend to get up early."

"Industrious."

"It is really more of a curse."

"Can I get you a Bloody Mary? Maybe a screwdriver?"

"Bloody Mary."

I settled into my regular booth and took the paperback from my coat pocket. I checked the copyright date: 1988. If Moon had only seen success with his recent string of progressively horrible books, this one must have tanked miserably. I began reading with low expectations, thinking perhaps Moon was not much of a writer after all. Perhaps he talked a good game, looked the part, but really was just a hack who had gotten lucky.

I was only a few paragraphs into the first chapter when I realized how wrong I had been. The prose was better, far better, than even the first I had read at the bookstore. The sheer mastery of language left me spellbound and I went from page to page, not noticing when the bartender set my drink in front of me.

"What's got your attention?"

I looked up with a flash of annoyance. I briefly displayed the book's cover.

"Ah, yes. Moon's first book."

"You know it?"

Archer grinned. "I'm not completely illiterate. I've read it more than once. Which may explain why I can't stomach that new stuff he's come out with."

"It seems to be popular."

"A lot of things are popular what shouldn't be. I'm no literary critic, but I can tell a difference between what you're reading and what he's published recently, even if I can't say exactly what that difference is."

"Do you know the story behind the change?"

"I know the story he's been telling people. How his publisher saddled him with a contract what robbed him of all artistic ability."

"Is that not true?"

"It's not the whole truth."

"What am I missing?"

The bartender preened his moustache. "Maybe you should talk to him."

"I think you know how he would take that."

"Still, I've already said more than a friend should."

"Are we not friends?"

"Doesn't give you access to another friend's privileged information. Enjoy your Bloody Mary."

I spent the rest of the morning at the Jesuit. I had lunch there, waiting for Moon to appear. But he never did. By three o'clock I was tired and closed out my tab.

I had devoured the book. As I walked back to my room, my thoughts were consumed with what I had read. The book was not just a masterpiece of prose. It was full of ideas and thematic material that investigated humanity. As ridiculous as I had always considered the term, it was nothing less than a contemporary classic, perhaps the best-kept secret in American literature over the last thirty years.

For the first time in months I needed a cigarette. I had quit cold turkey, one of my few triumphs, but now the urge was irresistible. I thought I remembered there being an old pack in the side pocket of my suitcase, leftover from a previous trip.

They were there. The pack was crumpled and the remaining cigarettes bent, but they should have still smoked. I reached in with two fingers and felt something else, something smaller and rolled roughly. I pulled out the joint and held it in my palm. This I had forgotten about. I placed it between my lips, but remembered I had no lighter. I considered using the hotel's clothes iron, but that seemed pathetic and dangerous. I was weighing the benefit of walking to a gas station when my room phone rang. I had forgot how strident that sound was and I answered with some degree of annoyance.

"It's Moon."

"Ah. How did you know where I was staying?"

"Small town. You can call every hotel in under ten minutes. They can be careless with customer privacy."

"I looked for you at the bar."

"Can't get enough of me, eh?"

"I just had a couple of questions," I said.

"Figures. Well, you're in luck. I had a couple of questions for you, too."

"Oh?"

"I read your book last night, the first one."

I paused.

"How did you manage that?"

"Online. It's on Kindle, you know."

"You read e-books?"

"It made me feel dirty, but I wanted to know what kind of

writer you are."

"What kind am I?"

"I think we should talk."

We made plans to eat dinner at the Jesuit and he hung up without saying goodbye.

* * *

It was understood we would sit at Moon's booth at the Jesuit and, although I would have preferred mine, I did not raise any objections. We ordered our usual drinks. They came and we ordered food. Moon got the rib eye. I opted for the house special: a towering, two patty bacon burger with cheese, called the Rosary.

Moon sampled his drink. "I've read your first book," he said, observing me over the rim of the glass.

"So you said on the phone."

"It was good. Damn good."

These words, coming from the man who had penned what I had read this morning, made me uneasy. I still had trouble accepting praise for that particular work. I deflected by mentioning I had read *The Lonely Peninsula*.

"So you found a copy?"

"The bookstore had one in the used book section."

"Ah."

"I was going to check the library, but they were closed."

"The snowstorm, yes. It wouldn't have done any good, as I don't believe they have a copy. Few were sold, really, and so they've become something of a collector's item. How much did the bookstore charge you?"

I stalled for time by taking a drink and pretending to check for the impending arrival of the food. "It was reasonable. But I would have paid much more. It is one of those books that makes me angry because I did not write it."

"Oh?" Moon's eyes lit up in a manner that seemed completely incongruous and foreign to him. It was almost a childlike reaction and I felt both drawn and repulsed by it. "You liked it, did you?"

"It was not so much a matter of liking the book," I said. "It was a matter of the book demanding to be liked. And liked is not even the right word. It was . . . well, it just was. The book spoke for itself. It did not *need* to be liked. It is one of those books that needs to be read."

"You're speaking of a classic."

"Indeed."

"High praise."

"And well deserved. I admit I had my doubts when I read some of the newer publications you have put your name to." I reached into my coat and pulled out the paperback. "But this won me over and removed all doubt. It showed me . . ." I trailed off. I had been about to say, "It showed me the kind of writer you used to be," but the words seemed cruel and, uncharacteristically, I cut them off as they teetered on my lips.

The food arrived and we began eating.

"Well, you've been incredibly kind," Moon said, "so let me return the favor. As I said, I read your book last night. Read it cover to cover in a single sitting, which is not something I typically do. It was well crafted, sensitive, deftly plotted, and taut. Not a wasted word or cloying sentiment to be found. It confirmed something I suspected last night."

"And what might that be?"

"That you're the one to write the final book of my contract."

I sat, stunned, drink in hand, and searched Moon's face for some sign of jest. But it was clear and free of guile. "You must be joking."

"Not at all. As I explained last night during that unusual

outburst of honesty, I'm at my wit's end with the entire venture. The strain has been too much for me. Perhaps if I were twenty years younger . . . but, no. It's taken me a great deal of soul-searching, but I now see and can admit that I need help. And after reading your book I think you're the one to do the helping."

"That book you read is years in the past," I said, fighting a rising sense of guilt. "How do you know I am still capable of turning out that caliber of work? One of the reasons I am even here is because I have constant difficulty with production."

"I'm convinced you just need the motivation," Moon said. "A writer doesn't lose that skill so quickly. Now me, I'm a different story. You're still on the rise. Last night I thought you might have peaked early, but now I see you are simply a talent in search of a vehicle. Think of me as your vehicle. Ghost write my final book and we'll both be free."

"How do you know your publisher will go for it?"

"They don't need to know. I can afford to pay you myself. Of course, your name will not be on the cover, but the money should allow you to live independently while you sort things out. From what you said last night your budget is on the lean side."

"Quite."

"We could help each other out."

I sat stunned, my thoughts a jumble, my emotions at odds. The thought of achieving financial stability was certainly appealing and I was flattered by such a vote of confidence. Writers were notoriously sensitive when it came to having others tamper with their work and here Moon was offering to let me write an entire book that would have his name emblazoned on the cover. Either he had immense confidence in me based on a single work or he was desperate enough to take the chance I would not turn out to be a bust. Or he simply did not care. The thought gave me pause. Perhaps he was so disgusted with his current situation he had little interest in whether or not the book was well written or well received. Additionally, I still had enough pride to resent the idea of doing work for which someone else would receive credit. I wanted to write something for myself, something that would catapult me back into the good graces of the reading public. And doing it as a ghost writer seemed an exercise in futility, at least in terms of that particular goal. But Moon was correct about one thing. The money would allow me to focus on writing. Not spending so much of my time writing shit pieces for quick cash would open up all manner of opportunities for pursuing something of real literary value. Another novel, perhaps. I could scrap the one on my computer and start from the beginning without fear of being late on the rent or running low on alcohol. At the same time, I could not escape the feeling that I would, in some way, be selling my artist's soul, indenturing myself to a master I knew very little about. Writing a novel was an arduous journey, not to be undertaken lightly. Giving that much of myself for the sake of another writer's book was not something I had ever seen myself doing. And how would I feel after it was over? Accomplished? Used? Suppose Moon's contract chewed me up and spit me out, as it had done to him? I certainly was not willing to ruin myself for someone else.

"What do you say?" Moon said. "It seems like it would work for both of us."

"I am going to have to think about it," I said. "It is a very generous offer; please do not consider me ungrateful if I ask for a little time."

Moon shifted. "Of course. I don't plan to leave town anytime soon. But don't take too long to decide. You're not the only writer in the game."

"You seem angry."

"Don't be ridiculous."

In my experience, anytime someone rebuffed a charge by

saying, "Don't be ridiculous," it meant the accuser was on to something. Moon's eyes had dimmed. His quickly negative reaction troubled me. If he was this easy to displease, what would it be like to work with him? And that raised another question: how much input and oversight of the project would he require? Would I be able to simply write and deliver or would he be over my shoulder for the duration? I did not work well under watchful eyes.

"Just give me a few days. A chance to think it over. This is no small thing you ask."

I looked at Moon and realized he was no longer listening to me. He stared over my shoulder toward the door, his face slack and eyes intense. I looked closer and saw what I can only describe as fear or, at least, trepidation. I leaned forward.

"Moon?" I placed a hand on his forearm, shook it gently. "Moon. Are you all right?"

A thin sheen of sweat appeared on his forehead and when he reached to wipe it away, he seemed to regain the present.

"Of course," he said. "A few days. You know where to find me."

He stood and left the bar, a little unsteadily, leaving me to pay the bill.

* * *

I stood in the snow next to my car. The tow truck man had called and said he was on the way. I had neglected to ask his estimated time of arrival, however, and "on the way" was clearly a highly adaptable term. Just as I was about to put in an angry call to his supervisor, a rattling, rusting behemoth of a vehicle tore into the parking lot and came to a halt, sliding sideways as it did so. The door opened with the shriek of cryptlike hinges and a tiny man in Carhartt coveralls dropped from the cab.

"You the fella with the dead battery?" He spoke loudly, almost yelling, as if unable to regulate his own decibel level.

"Yes. This is my car."

The little man swooped around to the driver's side and popped open the hood. A quick look at the engine elicited a raucous chortle.

"See anything?"

He peered around the open hood. "You check the engine before you called?"

"No. Should I have?"

"Most folks do."

"It never does me any good. What I know about the inner workings of automobiles would fit on a matchbook."

"Hah! Matchbook! That's a good one!" He wasted a full minute laughing and then wiped his eyes. "It looks like your battery got disconnected. I just hooked you back up. Give 'er a crank."

I slid onto the driver's seat and turned the key. The engine roared to life.

"Fuck."

"What's that, mister?" the man shouted.

"Nothing!" I shouted back. "Thanks for the help!"

"Hey, no problem! That'll be thirty bucks."

"Thirty?"

"Service call fee. Be glad I'm not chargin' you for the labor."

"La . . . labor? You hooked up a wire!"

"Don't get smart with me, fella," the little man said. "You thought this was free? I run a business, not a goddamn charity." All mirth had disappeared. Apparently he was only jolly outside of business negotiations.

"All right, all right. Here." I handed him a twenty and two fives as dismissively as possible.

He snatched the money and departed in a roar of indignation and diesel fumes.

I walked the short distance to the coffee shop and ordered a bagel and chai tea latte. I drank and thought about Moon's indecent, yet tempting proposal. As much as I wanted and needed the money, I did not want to tie myself to the whims of another writer. As a writer, I knew what that might entail. If I were another person, I would not want to work for myself. It would be a nightmare. But I had given myself a little time, more than enough to get well out of town before Moon knew I was gone. It would be easier to simply leave rather than explain why I was turning down the project. And I was unsure I would be able to resist the offer if I gave him another chance to convince me. But it was for the best.

I drained the tea and was about to head back to my room when I saw her. She sat across the room, holding a cup to her lips and smiling at me. Her red hair was pulled back in a style that revealed high cheekbones and accentuated deep blue eyes. The sight of her reminded me I had not enjoyed female companionship in . . . I tried to remember exactly how long, but could not. I ventured a return smile and she stood and walked toward my table. She was taller than expected and wore those tight black leggings that seemed so popular. Her top half was swathed in a long, loose-fitting sweater and sported a scarf tossed around her neck and shoulders with meticulous insouciance.

"I don't remember seeing you around here," she said. "Your first time?"

"No, I have been here several times. But I usually just pass through."

"You don't care for the town?"

"I think St. Francis is a fine town."

"Liar. Nobody likes St. Francis in the winter."

"Are you a local?"

"I am for now. What's your name, Mr. Passing Through?"

I told her. "And who might you be?"

"Kate. Where have I heard your name before?"

"Do you read novels by obscure writers?"

"Every chance I get." Her lips were glossy and red.

"Then that's probably where you heard my name. I wrote a book a few years ago. It hit a bestseller list or two."

"What are you doing now?"

"Having coffee with the loveliest girl in town."

"Oh, please. You can do better than that."

"I would not count on that."

"You could try, at least."

"Maybe. But I would need more time."

"A slow starter?"

"The slowest."

"Then I think we're going to need refills."

Over coffee and tea, we talked. Did we ever talk. Kate was remarkably knowledgeable on all things literary and I found myself enjoying not only her company but the conversation as well. She talked of Joyce and Faulkner, the Lost Generation, the Beats. Her favorite author was T.C. Boyle and she quoted Gabriel García Márquez. I wanted this woman.

We talked until it was dark outside and street lights came on. We talked until the barista said the shop was closing and then we stood outside in the cold.

"This has been nice," I said. "More than nice. It is not often I have such a fulfilling conversation."

"With the loveliest girl in town?"

"With anyone. You should not sell yourself short. You know more about books and writers than most writers of books."

"Now see there? I knew you could do better."

My heart clenched and I felt a trickle of sweat under my collar. "My room is in that hotel." I pointed.

She tilted her head and smiled. "Mr. Passing Through, are you inviting me up to your room?"

"Would you go?"

"You wouldn't think less of me?"

"I would not."

"I don't usually go to the rooms of strange men."

"Am I that strange?"

"You're a writer. Writers can be forgiven many things."

"I like the philosophy." I nodded toward the hotel. "My room is not far."

"Not far at all."

We walked through the snow and her hand found mine. It was warm and I grasped it like a lifeline. Once in my room I became more nervous. Kate looked around, appearing completely at ease.

"It's not bad, as far as hotel rooms go. Pretty standard." She sat down hard on the bed, testing its firmness. She looked up at me with a teasing half smile. "It doesn't squeak."

"That is a shame," I said, trying to match her sensuality. "How will the neighbors know?"

She fell backward on the bed and emitted a loud moan as if in the heat of sex, then looked at me for approval. "How was that? I can do better."

I sat down next to her. "Who are you?"

"Was that a rhetorical question?"

"Mostly."

"Just don't pinch yourself. Much too cliché."

"I would not dream of it."

"Funny."

"Shall we engage in foreplay?"

"I thought we just did." She grabbed the front of my shirt and pulled me into her. She was soft and knew what she was doing.

Afterward, I really wanted a smoke.

"Do you happen to have a light?"

She rummaged in her bag and came out with a Bic lighter. "You're a smoker? I thought smokers were a dying breed, a victim of the insufferable self-righteousness of a pseudo-socialistic society."

"We are dying, either from cancer or shame. I quit some time ago. I relapse under special circumstances."

"Am I to assume this is a special circumstance?"

"Indeed." I retrieved the crumpled pack of cigarettes and remembered the single joint. I pulled it out casually and placed it between my lips. I looked to see if Kate had noticed. She was watching, bemused.

"You're even more fun than I thought," she said.

"I suppose I should have asked if you are a cop."

"I would have thought our earlier conversation would have answered that."

"Of course, how silly of me." I lit the joint, took a drag, and offered it. "Care for a puff?"

She accepted, inhaled, coughed. "That's some funky shit."

"Sorry. It has been aging for some time."

"I'll say. If I'd known how the night would go down, I would have brought some decent weed."

"I admit to being a terrible host."

She rolled over to press against me. Her hand explored beneath the sheets. "You are an excellent host. I'm always more interested in the entertainment than the refreshments."

She pushed herself up and kissed me, and then slid out of bed and dressed slowly.

"You can stay," I said. "Have you seen the time?"

"I'm afraid if I stayed I wouldn't get much sleep. And, while that wouldn't be the worst thing, I do love my down time. Perhaps we can see each other again. When did you say you were leaving?"

I opened my mouth to say "tomorrow," but stopped. "I did not say, actually. The truth is, I do not know exactly. It depends on how things work out here."

"I see. Business in town?"

"Yes. Business."

"Well, here's to your business taking as long as we need it to." She gave me a single wink and left the room.

It may have been the pot. It may have even been the good mood caused by post-coitus. Whatever the reason, I lay in bed after Kate's departure rethinking Moon's offer. I now had reason to stay in town even longer, a flagrant violation of my ritual. But I would not be able to avoid Moon for long. Additionally, I would not be able to hold Kate's interest by continuing the bare bones existence I was now living. Eating and drinking at the Jesuit every day would severely deplete my budget and I doubted a girl like that would be interested in spending each night sitting in my hotel room and eating ramen. For that matter, I would not be able to retain this room for too long. The thought of leaving St. Francis was dropping quickly on my list of priorities. But my ability to stay would soon be severely compromised. Moon had said he would advance me enough money to live on while the book was written. With that cash flow, I could pursue Kate and write the book that might put me back in the game.

I shook my head and tried to puff the joint, but found it had burned out. Was I really considering changing my entire plan because of a single sexual experience? Was I that pathetic and desperate? But I could not escape the thought that Kate was unlike any girl I had ever met. I had read that in books and seen it in movies, and always considered it a silly plot device. Now I was faced with just such a reality and it was not silly at all. It was reality. We shared similar interests, she was well read, she could fuck better than anyone I had ever shared a bed with, and she seemed to be into me. I would not be at all surprised to find she wrote her own material. The thought of sharing the craft with someone like her filled me with longing.

I pushed down into the bed until I was supine and looked up at the ceiling. My life was complicating quickly. And complications were things I went to great lengths to avoid, even enduring other complications to circumvent the original ones. Kate was one complication I felt willing to accept. Even if it meant changing my ritual.

The ceiling was white plaster, with patterns troweled in for decoration. As I watched, the weaving lines began moving back and forth, serpentine movements that turned them into actual snakes crawling on the ceiling and coming down the walls. They fell to the floor with little plopping sounds, curling and coiling, wrapping themselves around each other. They seemed to divide and multiply like cells going through mitosis and soon surrounded the bed. My mouth was dry. I pushed upright in the bed, trying to put distance between myself and the growing abomination on the floor. I realized I still held the cold joint and quickly dropped it onto the bedside table. Kate was right. That was some funky shit. The snakes were long, thin, black, and when they opened to hiss and spit I saw the deep blood red of their mouths. Fangs dripped with venom and seemed to vibrate with toxicity, eager to sink into my quivering, crawling flesh. It was then I noticed how dark it had become. The bedside lamp still shone, but its light seemed filtered. The entire room was dim, as though I were wearing sunglasses or it was hazy with smoke. I pulled myself into the smallest space possible, arms wrapped around knees that pressed into my chin. The first snake head appeared over the foot of the bed. It looked at me with black, glistening eyes and flicked its tongue. It hated me. The long, scaly-smooth body oozed onto the bed, losing itself among the tousled sheets that so recently had witnessed such pleasure. The current horror soiled even that memory. The snake was only a couple of feet away and already I could see others moving up the sides of the bed. It drew back, coiled, hissed, its head bobbing back and forth like a boxer in the ring. I got my feet underneath me and jumped as far toward the door as possible. The mattress did not make the best launching pad, but I made it almost halfway. Even so, I came down on a twisting, writhing pile of snakes. I felt the bottom of my feet crush them and slide over their scales. They were more slippery than I would have expected. I knew if I fell they would be all over me in seconds. I made another jump for the door, grasped the handle, and threw it open. I staggered into the hallway, almost falling to my knees, and saw a Hispanic woman pushing a cart loaded with fresh towels and supplies. She stared at me in horror. I was naked and screaming about snakes. I looked back into the room and was both relieved and humiliated to see nothing amiss. No snakes, no shadowy atmosphere. Nothing but the faint odor of ancient marijuana hanging in the air like a sign around my neck that said, "druggie."

"Please," I said, reaching toward the cleaning woman. She shrank away and grabbed a bottle of cleaning solution.

"Stay back," she said, her pronunciation poor. "I will spray!"

"I am not going to hurt you. I was . . . having a bad dream."

"Stay back!"

I retreated back into my room and slammed and locked the door. I leaned against it, the metal surface cool against my naked back. I closed my eyes and breathed deeply, trying to calm the pounding in my ears. I knew I needed help. The hallucinations were becoming worse. What if I had one while driving in heavy traffic or saw something that caused me to inflict harm on another person? But seeking treatment was not an option. Besides the cost involved, I would not do anything that might involve being locked away in a facility. I knew too much about them to ever risk it.

I pushed away from the door and went to shower. I hoped the water would not turn to blood.

Part Two

Growing up in northern Michigan, I had water and woods in my blood. Spending days by the various lakes and ponds that dotted the area was a common pastime, but I had my favorites. The one I visited the most was Mosquito Bay and today it lay quiet and flat like glass. In addition to being too early for tourist season, this particular body of water was not often frequented by locals. Perhaps the name was partially responsible; just because the mosquito happened to be the Michigan state bird did not mean anyone wanted to visit a place named after it. And it was not exceptional in most other ways. It did not have the best fishing or the best swimming. It had no beach to speak of, just a single, ancient pier that looked as if it might collapse into the water at the slightest provocation. It was not particularly close to the main road, nor did it have a dedicated campground. In fact, the land immediately surrounding the water tended to be soft and marshy. It was not even technically a bay, since it was surrounded on all sides by land. And yet, late in the day, when the heavy sun began to sink into that giant pool of fire known as Lake Michigan, Mosquito Bay came alive in sound and color. A symphony of crickets and frogs serenaded a stunning light show of reds, oranges, and golds that streaked across a placid surface of water broken only by the minute pinpricks of scooting pond skimmers. It was an experience that typified a Michigan summer night: the tickle of humidity on the back of the neck, the whine of a mosquito in the ear.

It was too early for all of this heaven. While the dogwoods bloomed in Chattanooga, there were patches of snow in Serenity, and the water temperatures were much too low for swimming. The breeze, although it smelled like spring, still carried a chill that cut through my shirt. I walked onto the pier and listened to it creak under my weight. I lay on my stomach with my head over the end of the pier and gazed down at my reflection. The boards of the pier were cool and rough and pressed hard against my chest. Past my head, far above me, the sky repeated itself. It was light blue, dotted with clouds, infinite.

Small bubbles floated to the surface of the water and floated there, a product of decomposition on the lake floor. I reached down and poked one of the bubbles. It instantly disappeared, just like that, and I wondered if that was how God viewed us. Like bubbles. One poke and *poof!* We are gone. Of course, there was no God. I had recently become convinced of this. At fifteen, I prided myself on being the youngest atheist I knew. In fact, given my insular lifestyle inside the world of Christ's Apostles Church, I was the *only* atheist I knew. Even my friend Nick, who was more than happy to deviate from the straight and narrow, was not yet willing to dismiss the idea of a heavenly being.

I still remember how it happened. I had always had questions, but still believed in God. In my world, that was something that did not even need to be discussed. Then I read a news report about a giant storm somewhere in Asia that killed thousands of people. The report included a series of graphic photos and heart-wrenching personal accounts of disaster and loss. I decided no loving God would let that happen and, if he did, I wanted nothing to do with him. That day, I decided to be an atheist and sought out books by the foremost atheist writers of the day. I even did some writing of my own on the subject. I had to read on the sly, of course, as my parents would have gone into convulsions, immediately followed by an intense period of prayer, had they known of my reading list. They considered my writing to be a waste of time, no matter what the topic.

As it was, the drama had to wait until I had informed them of my new status, an unwise move that occurred in the heat of an argument. Upon hearing the news of my apostasy, my mother dissolved into tears. I was banished to my room until I had memorized key passages of Scripture, such as Psalm 33:6—*"By the word of the Lord were the heavens made, and all the host of them by the breath of His mouth"*—and Hebrews 11:6—*"But without faith it is impossible to please Him. For he that cometh to God must believe that He is, and that He is a rewarder of those who diligently seek Him."* Then my father, the pastor of Christ's Apostles, had called up every church member and requested prayer. And so it was I became known as the resident atheist and the constant subject of every prayer meeting since.

I shifted on the pier until my feet hung in the water. I had not taken off my shoes and the cold wetness took a moment to seep between the stitching and under the laces. When it finally did, the coldness made my toes tingle. It was almost painful, but felt good at the same time.

I still thought about God and religion. It was impossible not to, being forced to attend church three times a week. I actually thought it would be something if God did exist and ended up being a little naïve or just really bad at his job. It would certainly explain a few things. It would have been refreshing to hear someone from the church toss out the old, tired rhetoric about original sin and free will, and be forced to say something like, "Right, so he meant well . . . it's just that he doesn't always understand how the real world works." The idea made me smile. A year or two ago, I would have worried such thoughts might send me to hell. I did not feel that fear anymore.

I moved forward and felt the cold water rise up my legs and soak the bottom of my pants. I shivered, partly from the chill, partly from pleasure. The feeling was so intense, painful even, it made everything seem clearer. It was good to feel. I looked at the quiet water near the center of the lake and at the surrounding shoreline, and it was as if I had been viewing the world through a diffusion filter that had fallen away, allowing the world to come suddenly into focus.

I once told a girl I liked about my hell theory and she went home crying. She later said she could not be around someone who hated God, but that she would be praying for me daily. I told her I did not hate God. I just wondered if he actually existed and, if he did, questioned his sanity. She told me questioning God was the same as denying Jesus. I tried calling her the next week and her mom answered the phone and called me "a wicked child" and forbade me to ever contact her daughter again.

The water had soaked my jeans halfway up my calves. My feet were no longer cold. In fact, they now felt almost warm. I wriggled forward on the pier and slowly lowered myself into the lake. Soon, the water was up to my waist. Gentle waves caused by the disturbance licked at my chest and soaked my shirt. The fabric clung to my body with an uncomfortable, clammy, bone-chilling tenacity. The lower half of me, the part under the water, felt calm and serene. Water had always held a strange dread for me; since I had been eight years old my father had pushed for baptism. I always pleaded off, being terrified of going underwater. But now I was not afraid. The water was the only place I wanted to be.

I heard a shout from shore and turned my head to see a man, probably in his fifties, standing just outside the brush line. He wore camouflage pants, a bright orange hat and vest, and cradled a shotgun in his right arm. He cupped his hands around his mouth to act as a megaphone. He was probably hunting wild turkeys, although he was a couple of days early.

"Water's too cold for swimmin'!" he shouted. "Get on outta there!"

I hung on the edge of the pier and looked back at him. I felt entirely composed and in control, unusual for me. I closed my eyes and concentrated on the strange warmness of my legs. It was as if I were in bed with the blankets pulled up to my waist and, for a moment, I thought I could reach down and pull the water blankets over my head. The thought made me sleepy and I wondered at the sudden feeling of fatigue that washed over me. I felt the water rising, blankets being pulled up to my neck and then over my head and then everything was quiet, like someone had muted the world. I heard a gurgling sound in my ears. Something had me by the arms. I heard a rush of noise as my head broke the surface of the water. Something pulled at me roughly. I must have struggled because it told me to be still. Then I was on solid ground with the side of my face pressed against cold, wet grass and throwing up lake water. My skin was so cold it burned and my teeth chattered so hard I thought they might splinter.

"Stop struggling," someone said. "Put this coat on."

I must have blacked out, because it seemed only an instant later I was being lifted into the back of an ambulance. The paramedics were asking me questions and I heard myself answer them in a voice that did not sound like my own. I felt disconnected, as if I were watching the entire scene unfold on a movie screen. For a brief moment, I wondered if I had died. Then I decided heaven would not be this unpleasant and hell would be a lot worse.

So I must still be alive, on Earth with all its mediocrity.

The news of my suicide attempt made waves both at church and throughout the town of Serenity. Of course, all news made quick rounds through Serenity. Its five thousand residents had little else to do. The stalwart members of Christ's Apostles were convinced God was convicting my soul and, heartened by the idea I was miserable enough to take my own life, redoubled their efforts to pray down God's judgment. My father, as pastor, missed no opportunity to suggest as much, even taping photocopied bits of Scripture to my bedroom door, verses that foretold the eventual destruction of all wayward humans. At the dinner table, the ritual meal prayer would include an explicit request to God for the salvation of my soul, after which I would be served food with the long-suffering attitude of a good Samaritan giving sustenance to all, regardless of merit. I knew God had nothing to do with my flirtation with drowning. It had not been God or even my disbelief in God. As such, I continued on my prodigal path and tried to ignore the relentless pressure being brought to bear.

* * *

My mother's voice stabbed through the warm June air. It scored a direct hit on my eardrum and rattled around inside my head, turning my brain to milk gravy. I squeezed my eyes shut to rid my mind of her piercing voice. She had grown up on a hog farm and I had heard relatives reminisce about her hog-calling capabilities when she was a girl. I had no doubts regarding any of these stories. I pressed my back against the rough wood of the shed wall and shifted just a little to let the stream of dust-infused light that sifted through the lone window play across the pages of the book I was reading.

> "Here," said Milady, rising with the majesty of a queen, "here, Felton, behold the new martyrdom invented for a pure young girl, the victim of the brutality of a villain. Learn to know the heart of men, and henceforth make yourself less easily the instrument of their unjust vengeance." Milady, with a rapid gesture, opened her robe, tore the cambric that covered her bosom, and red with feigned anger and simulated shame, showed the young man the ineffaceable impression that dishonored that beautiful shoulder.

My mother called again. I calculated the tone in her voice. Judging from its pitch and volume, I figured to have enough time to finish the page and possibly the next. I did not know what cambric was, but assumed it was some kind of undergarment. I squeezed my eyes shut and imagined Milady's breasts aglow in lamplight, nipples hard and sharp. This was a book I could show my friend Nick. We had a standing agreement to let each other know whenever we came across a salacious passage in an acceptable book. I felt a thrill between my legs and kept reading.

> "So beautiful! so young!" cried Felton, covering that hand with his kisses.
>
> Milady let one of those looks fall upon him which make a slave of a king.
>
> Felton was a Puritan; he abandoned the hand of this woman to kiss her feet. He no longer loved her; he adored her.
>
> When this crisis was past, when Milady appeared to have resumed her self-possession, which she had never lost; when Felton had seen her recover with the veil of chastity those treasures of love which were only concealed from him to make him desire them the more ardently, he said—

She called again, and her tone had escalated faster than I had anticipated. I folded down the corner of the page and closed the book. I heard the back door slam and knew she was coming down the steps to the yard. I scrambled to my feet, brushed the back of my pants with one hand, and ducked out the side door of the shed toward the house, the book held close and partially covered with my hand.

She was heading toward the end of the yard near the wood line when she saw me. She stopped walking and stood, hands on hips. Her hair was worn pulled back straight and her face, unadorned by cosmetics, was stern.

"I've been calling for you. Didn't you hear me?"

"Not until just now. Sorry."

"What've you been up to?" She was like a drug-sniffing dog when it came to guilt.

I shrugged. "Nothing. Just reading."

She saw the book. "What is that?"

I handed it over. She stood for a moment, silently critiquing the cover.

"*The Three Musketeers*. Haven't read it myself. Is it appropriate for a Sunday?"

"It's a classic," I said.

The church's standing on entertainment, such as reading, was quite clear in that it should all be for the glory of God. Otherwise, it was frivolous and likely sinful. At the very least, it took one's mind away from important spiritual things. Being of the opinion the modern age was almost entirely to blame for the degradation of humanity, however, they did consider classics largely acceptable. It was fortunate my mother, along with most of the rest of the church, was not widely read and therefore did not know anything about Dumas's penchant for mentioning Milady de Winter's "treasures."

My mother took the book from me and turned it over in her hands. I held my breath. She opened it, scanned a few lines, and then handed it back, watching me carefully for signs of nervousness or lust.

"Well, I guess it's okay. Anything that old is probably okay." She continued watching me as she spoke. She was suspicious. She could smell the guilt, but could not discern the source. "Get washed up for dinner."

I helped set the table and then my mother called downstairs to my father's study, telling him dinner was ready. As he made his way up the stairs, they creaked and cracked in protest. My father preached against many sins, but gluttony was suspiciously absent. He was a man with two passions, food and Scripture, and he consumed them both with equal voracity. His enjoyment of food was made obvious by the ampleness of a stomach that always entered a room before he did. While it was impossible for my father to have an actual beer belly, as he eschewed all use of alcohol, he made up for it by ingesting all manner of other things bad for the health. My father would eat fried gravy if he could get someone to make it for him.

He sat down in his customary place at the head of the table. The chair squeaked and shifted ominously, as if trying to wriggle from underneath its crushing burden. He placed his hands in the classic prayer pose and my mother and I followed suit. As a form of silent protest, I kept my eyes open.

"Dear Heavenly Father," he prayed, "bless this food and the hands that prepared it. Help us all to live within your favor and avoid anything that would separate us from your protection. Give me the wisdom to lead this family, give my wife the grace to follow your footsteps, and give my son an understanding of the folly of his ways. Show him that you are real, Father. Make him sick for God. Turn him from his wicked unbelief and back toward you. In Jesus's name we pray, amen."

My mother began passing the food.

"Don't forget we have church tonight," my father said through a mouthful of instant mashed potatoes.

"Yes, we do," my mother said. She looked at me. "And that is why we can't have you dillydallying around. We're already a little late eating."

"Maybe I could stay home tonight," I said. I knew it was hopeless, but that never stopped me from trying. "I'm not feeling all that great."

"What's wrong with you?" my father asked.

"Just a headache. And my stomach is a little upset."

"You'll be fine."

"But I really don't feel well."

"You're going."

"Perhaps if he doesn't feel well—"

My mother broke off as my father's open palm smacked the table top.

"I won't be questioned in my own house! He's going!"

"Yes, dear." My mother looked as meek as a puppy caught eating steak from the table. Now I actually did feel unwell. Watching my mother bullied into submission was a familiar sight, but one that never ceased to sicken me.

The church parking lot was already full of cars by the time my mother pulled the tan Toyota Corolla into a spot. She got out and looked back impatiently. I had gotten my arm stuck in the seatbelt. She did not actually start tapping her foot, but I could tell she wanted to. I had dawdled too long at home and my father ended up having to take his old truck, leaving me and my mother to come later.

"Now you've made us late," my mother said. She hated being late to any place, but church was the worst of all. She was the pastor's wife. What would people say? I could hear the music already starting, the piano and organ—the only instruments allowed—playing "Nothing but the Blood." I managed to disentangle myself and we power walked into church and took a seat in the back row. My mother hated sitting in the back row. The back row was for people who planned to make a quick getaway in the event of an unexpected altar call. The pastor's family had a designated pew at the front. I looked around for Nick and saw him trying to catch my eye. He was sitting with his family in their usual place. They had not been late. He grinned at me and mouthed the words, *Haha, you're late.*

I rolled my eyes in an attempt to communicate my belief that being late for church was not such a big deal. He mouthed something else, but I could not make it out.

What?

Meet me after church. He pointed downstairs.

I knew what he meant. The church used to operate on a well before it had been connected to the city water supply and the well access room still existed behind the furnace. It was a cramped space, accessible only by a small opening in the cement block wall, but was the perfect hiding spot for us. The only other person who even knew about the well room was the caretaker and, now that water was supplied by the city, there was no reason for him to go back there. When we discovered the room a couple of years ago, we had taken a pledge to guard the secret with our lives. Now that we were older, we thought the pledge was dumb, but still were careful not to be seen either entering or exiting.

I felt a rap on my knuckles and looked up to see my mother frowning down at me. I glanced over at Nick to give him a "this is your fault" stare, but he was looking straight ahead, looking as pious as hell.

The introductory music ended and the song leader rose to call out the first congregational hymn. The proceedings were always the same. You could set a watch by it. I made a mental checklist and marked off the events as they happened. First song, check. Second song, check. Prayer, check. Third song, check. Special music (a solo by a man who badly impersonated Tennessee Ernie Ford), check. Offering, check. Finally the sermon came and I was lulled into a state of dull semiconsciousness by the voice of my father.

The sound of my father's Bible popping shut brought me around and I looked up, eagerly awaiting the benediction. Instead, he paused and cleared his throat.

"I have been carrying a burden for this church for several years," he said, "and I feel that it is in need of a spiritual renewal."

He paused. The crowd was completely silent, waiting, holding its collective breath.

"That is why I have scheduled a revival meeting for our church, so that we can renew our faith and dedication to God. Now, some of you might not have been attending here when we had our last revival, so let me tell you what that is. A revival is an intense period of soul-searching and prayer. A time when we can come together as a church to seek the mind of God, and to pray for those loved ones not yet safe within the will of our Heavenly Father. Now usually we have a special speaker come in for these events, but we have specific needs in our church that an outsider would not understand. For that reason, I have decided to preach the sermons myself. Services will be held every night for a week, beginning in three weeks. I realize this is short notice, but it's what God has laid on my heart."

"Can you fucking believe it?" Nick asked once we were safely ensconced in the well room. "A fucking revival?"

"Fuck me," I said, shaking my head and putting one hand to

my brow as if feeling for a fever. "Like we have time in the summer to spend in fucking church."

We spoke in half whispers to keep our profanity-laced voices from wafting up through the stairwell. There were times when I waited all week to be able to use ungodly language and was always eager to try out any new combinations I had either heard or devised on my own.

"Goddamn motherfucking revival," I experimented. It sounded good—good and badass.

"You said it," Nick said.

I noticed he did not repeat the words and felt a little thrill. Apparently, Nick had not yet graduated to "motherfucking." I smiled. Nick realized I had noticed his omission and reddened. He turned to a raggedy cardboard box in the corner and rummaged inside. He came up with something behind his back, a look of triumph on his still flushed face.

"So what do you have for me?" he asked. "Find anything good this week?"

I shrugged. "Not really. It looks like you did, though. What do you have there?"

"Ah, nothing. What did you find?"

I handed him the copy of *The Three Musketeers* with the steamier passages bookmarked and underlined. He scoffed.

"That's nothing." He handed the book back and then, with a low bow and a grand gesture, pulled a glossy magazine from behind his back. "Check this out."

I looked at the cover and instantly felt hardness between my legs. A sultry brunette stood like a giantess wearing only a red, white, and blue string bikini that looked as if it might fly off at any moment and take someone's eye out. Her breasts tested the limits of their restraints and I thought I could see a tiny fringe of pubic hair around the outline of the bikini bottoms. I gaped in appreciative wonder. "Where'd you get this?"

Nick smirked. "My brother came home last week."

"He gave this to you?"

"Fuck, yeah. He has a whole collection of *Playboy* and had a duplicate. So he gave the extra to me."

Nick's brother Seth lived in Los Angeles. An unrepentant sinner for years, he had gone to Hollywood to try for the movies. He came home every once in a while when he ran short of money for devil weed, or so my mother told me. I thought Seth sounded like a lot of fun, although I had not seen him in years and barely remembered him.

"Do your parents know?"

"About the magazine? Shit, no! That's why I'm leaving it here. When Seth's home, my mom checks my room every now and then for contraband. This isn't the first time Seth has brought me awesome stuff from LA, so she's suspicious. If I kept this at my place, she'd find it for sure. Does your mom check your room?"

"I don't think so," I said. "But I'm pretty careful not to leave stuff where she could find it. She doesn't know much about books and as long as it doesn't have a racy cover and was written prior to 1960, she doesn't usually suspect much."

"You're lucky," Nick said. "My mom taught English at a college before she got saved and married my dad, so she knows what to look for. Although, after this," he indicated the *Playboy*, "some of that other stuff doesn't seem so special."

I had to agree. I stood there with the Dumas book in my hand, feeling foolish and one-upped. My "motherfucking" paled in comparison to the bikini-clad woman on the *Playboy* cover. I cast my pride, and the book, aside and reached for the magazine.

"Let me see it." I could only imagine what wonders awaited inside. Talk about treasures!

Nick pulled it away. "Not so fast. I haven't even looked through it all yet. I almost got caught with it at home just before we left for church, so I can't risk taking it back. You have to promise not to tell anyone about this."

I felt hurt. This was not something we even had to mention. Discretion was simply understood when it came to the secret room and all that went on there. Our safety was secure through the beauty of mutually assured destruction.

"Of course I'm not going to tell," I said. "Shit, man."

"Sorry. I've just been kinda nervous about this whole thing lately."

"What thing?"

"The room and everything. I think my parents suspect something, especially my mom. And it doesn't help that we're having a revival. You ever been to a revival?"

I nodded. "A couple of times. They were pretty intense."

"Shit."

"Yeah," I said. "Shit."

* * *

Throughout the first half of that week, I could think of nothing but the *Playboy*. I lay awake at night thinking of the patriotic woman, unable to sleep, and imagining what might be between the glossy covers. It was not the first time I had seen a picture of a naked woman. Every now and then a guy at school would show up with a photograph or a magazine, but that was mostly it. It was much more challenging for me to find such things than it was for my more informed acquaintances. The few secular friends I had always laughed at how difficult it was for me to find this type of commodity.

My existence without these simple pleasures seemed pathetic and my worldly friends agreed. They could not comprehend the austerity of Christ's Apostles Church, which held to a "high standard of holiness" as taught by early preachers like John Wesley. Of course, certain things did not exist back when John Wesley was alive and coming up with ways to make people miserable, so Christ's Apostles tended to be technologically backward. They always erred on the side of deprivation. If unsure concerning the godliness of something, they eschewed it just in case. The television, for example, was met with frosty disapproval. This puritanical stance did nothing for my popularity among those of my age group. Even my religious friends at private school had a difficult time believing I lived without television. They were always asking me if I had seen last night's episode of the popular new show, which of course I had not.

As the week dragged by, my eagerness to get to church in order to finally crack open the cover of the *Playboy* was tempered by my growing dread of the revival. My mother was nearly giddy with excitement and I could hear her praying every night for the redemption of those church members whose souls she felt might be in jeopardy. I was surprised at the length of the list, but assumed she was simply being cautious.

I was also suffering from insomnia, as the minx from the *Playboy* cover continued to haunt my nights. By Wednesday, I was exhausted from lack of sleep and rode my bike into Serenity to meet Nick at the ice cream shop. When I arrived, I saw he had brought Seth along. I felt a little awestruck. This was the guy who had left home for the city of depravity and come back bearing the gift that now waited for me in the church well room.

Nick saw me ride up and waved wildly. He was practically peeing his pants with excitement over reacquainting me with Seth.

"You remember Seth?"

I nodded. "A little."

Seth stuck out his hand. "Nice to see ya, kid. Nick says you liked the magazine I sent over."

I felt my face turn red like a party balloon.

Seth laughed. "I'll take that as a yes."

"You don't have to worry about Seth," Nick said. "He's cool. I've told him everything. He says we're hilarious."

"You told him everything?"

"Yeah." Nick nodded. "Don't worry. He won't tell. Will you, Seth?"

Seth shook his head and made a zipping motion over tightly compressed lips. "Nada wordo," he said. "Your secret's safe with me."

We got our ice cream and sat outside to eat.

Seth looked around, a wry smile on his face. "Ah, the old town," he said with a wistful tone I suspected was bogus. He pointed across the street. "Who are those assholes?"

I followed his gaze and saw a straggly group of kids walking on the other side of the street. "That's Mitch Tolliver and his gang."

Seth laughed. "Wait . . . Serenity has a gang? What's the requirement for membership, diapers? Do those kids even shave yet?"

"In order to join, you have to be held back at least two grades." Nick chuckled. "It's like the opposite of Mensa."

"Wow. Just . . . wow. I've been in LA too long, I guess. I'm used to seeing actual gangs, the kind who would rip out your fingernails with rusty pliers if you didn't pay your drug bill."

"Tolliver's gang mostly spray paints the war memorial and eggs houses on Halloween," I said. "If they get ambitious, they might steal a car now and then."

"Why don't the cops just break them up?" Seth asked.

"Mitch's dad is the new sheriff."

"Well, fuck," Seth said.

"So what've you been doing?" Nick asked me. "Praying up for

the revival?"

Seth laughed.

I sighed. "Nah. My mom has that covered. I've been too exhausted to do much."

"Is she keeping you up at night?"

"Who?"

"Your mom. With her praying."

"Oh! No. I thought you meant the woman on the magazine cover." I glanced around to make sure we were out of earshot of anyone I knew. "It's driving me crazy! I can't sleep at night and my crotch is starting to hurt." I stuck my tongue against the side of my Superman ice cream cone and twirled it. I often found myself attempting to achieve equal distribution and tended to strive for symmetry. At school, I kept identical pencils, one on either side of my desk. I would alternate the sharpening to make sure one did not become noticeably shorter than the other. When they both became too short to use comfortably, I walked to the wastebasket and threw them away at the same time. I received a fair amount of teasing for this habit and I could not explain why I did it. It was just something I needed to do. And if I tried not to, I always felt anxious, as if something bad was about to happen because of my negligence.

"I have the same problem sometimes," Nick said. "It sucks."

Seth let out a long sigh. "You two are fucking pathetic."

"Fuck you," Nick said. "Why do you say that?"

"It's a simple problem with an even simpler solution," Seth said. "You both just need to jerk off. Don't tell me neither of you know how to jerk off."

"Jerk what off?" Nick asked.

Seth sighed. "I've really failed you, little brother. I'm talking about your wiener, your rod, your one-eyed snake. Your fucking penis!"

I felt a light bulb begin to glow inside my head. It was a dim light bulb, but a light bulb just the same. "That's why I can't sleep?"

"No question," Seth said. "Jesus, the church really did a number on you guys, didn't it? Listen, you two little numb nuts, guys get backed up with jizz after a while and it gives us blue ball syndrome."

These were new terms to me. "Jizz?"

"Sperm. The stuff that makes babies. You know how babies are made, right?"

The concept was fuzzy. I knew no storks were involved, but that was about it. "Of course I do. I just didn't know the word."

"Right," Seth said, his tone suggesting he could see right through me. "In any case, every now and then, you just have to grab your dick and rub one out. You'll feel way better, trust me." He took a big bite of ice cream. Apparently, he had no obsessive-compulsive tendencies. "Oh, and don't believe that shit about jerking off making you go blind," he said through a mouthful of dairy. "The fucking church just made that up to scare people. Sometimes I choke the bishop twice a day and I still see fine."

"Seth wants to see the well room," Nick said.

I squirmed. Telling Seth about the room was one thing; taking him to see it was quite another. I felt a surge of resentment against Nick for what was amounting to a full-fledged betrayal. Seth was not likely to let the word out, but it was still against our plan to keep the room an absolute secret. Nick had said last Sunday he was feeling more nervous with our secrets, so why was he now so keen to share them?

"I don't know," I said. "We were going to keep all that a secret. You know, between us."

"Aw, come on, kid," Seth said. "I haven't seen the old church in years. And I'm certainly not going on a Sunday. I'll just be in and out."

I gave up. It was clear they were going to do whatever they wanted anyway. Nick worshipped his brother and was clearly capable of treachery if he thought it would make Seth think more highly of him.

"Fine," I said. "Okay. But how are we going to get in? The church is always locked during the day."

"Leave that to me," Seth said ominously.

The ride to the church took less than fifteen minutes. Serenity is not a large town and, if it were a few miles farther east, would be nothing more than an extension of Traverse City. As it was, it occupied a tiny, independent dot on the Michigan map. Most of the town's income was related to tourism, as several wealthy families had built vacation homes on area lakes. The location gave them access to the amenities and attractions of Traverse City without the constant hassle of the millions of tourists who visited the area each year.

The church building—an old structure with whitewashed, wooden siding and black shingled roof—was quiet when we rolled into the parking lot. Seth rode around to the far side of the building, the one out of sight from the street, before stopping his bike. He let the bike fall to the ground and began walking along the side wall, trying the line of windows as he went.

"What's he doing?" I whispered to Nick.

Nick shrugged. "Trying to find an unlocked window, I guess."

The windows were all locked, but he paused at the side door and began messing with the lock with something taken from his pants pocket. A few minutes later, after much profanity from Seth and nervous fidgeting from me and Nick, there was a click and Seth pushed the door open. He gave us thumbs up and waved us forward. This all seemed like an extremely bad idea. The phrase "breaking and entering" kept coming to mind and I could not help but wonder how massive a stroke my father would have if he ever found out I had broken into a church. And not just any church, but *his* church: the holiest, most godly church in Serenity.

Nick and I stood in the deserted sanctuary, shuffling our feet and looking around furtively. Even though I was an atheist, I felt God watching us. The giant backlit cross that hung on the wall behind the pulpit seemed to pulse, as if trying to send me a message. It was like I had broken into the tomb of Jesus on the second day.

Seth strode forward, but even he was affected. "Nothing creepier than an empty church," he said. He stepped onto the platform and peered behind the pulpit where the offering plates were kept.

I leaned toward Nick. "What's he doing?"

Nick shrugged, a look of intense apprehension on his face.

Seth pulled out the offering plates and held them aloft. Even from my vantage point, I could see they were full of bills and money envelopes.

"I can't believe they still don't lock this shit up!" Seth said, grinning. His voice echoed through the sanctuary as if it were a cave fitted with padded benches.

"It kinda *was* locked up," I muttered.

Nick elbowed me hard in the ribs. "Shut up! He'll hear you!"

Seth was rifling through the plates and opening the money envelopes, picking out the cash and dropping the checks back in.

"Maybe he *should* hear me. He's stealing money from the church!"

"Since when do you care about the church?"

"It's not that. It's just—" I stopped before saying some of the money belonged to my parents, who could not afford everything they gave to the church, to say nothing of having it ripped off by some California transplant pothead.

Seth folded a stack of bills and shoved it into his pocket. He jumped off the platform and grinned at us. "Not a lot of big denominations, but worth the trip. Thanks, little brother." He reached back into his pocket and pulled out a couple of five-dollar bills. He handed one to Nick and one to me. "Consider that your commission." He looked as if he had just given us the donation that would allow us to have a life-saving operation. "So where's this secret room you guys are so proud of?"

If I had been uncertain about showing Seth the room before, I was even more so now. At least we did not have anything valuable down there. Nothing except the *Playboy* he had given us. I wondered if he would decide he wanted it back.

Nick led the way downstairs to the well room. Seth had a little extra trouble squeezing into the tight space, but he finally managed to scramble through. It was a tight fit inside the room with a third person.

"So this is it, huh," Seth said. "Doesn't look like much."

"Yeah, it's kinda shitty," Nick said.

I wanted to punch the little ass kisser right in the face. I supposed I should not be so pissed off at Nick, just because he was trying to get on his brother's good side, but it felt like he was throwing both me and our friendship under the bus.

"I like it," I said. "It's like the Underground Railroad or a secret hiding room during World War II."

"Whatever, man," Seth said. "What's in the box?"

Nick opened the box and took out our paltry collection of semierotic material.

Seth took one look at the pile of marginally racy classics, topped by the single *Playboy* magazine, and let out a single harsh guffaw.

"You guys are fucking pathetic!" he snorted. He turned to Nick. "This is your stash? You led me to believe you had some hot stuff down here."

Nick wilted under his brother's mockery and looked so dismal I began to pity him.

"We don't have a lot of sources," I said. "We have to get our stuff wherever we can."

"I'll give you points for being resourceful," Seth said, grabbing the *Playboy*, "but, shit, this is bad." He opened the magazine to its center and shook it. I gaped as the connected pages cascaded down, revealing a stunningly naked woman. Seth held it up in front of us. "Okay, so you two are complete fucking losers, but I'm going to help you. Drop your pants."

We both looked at him, bewildered and shocked.

"Do what?" we both asked.

"Drop your fucking pants! Come on. I don't have all day. I'm going to show you how to jerk off. You can't go on keeping it all bottled up. It's not healthy."

Nick and I looked at each other. Slowly, embarrassed but intensely curious, we unzipped.

"Your underwear, too, idiots." Seth rolled his eyes and muttered, "I've got my fucking work cut out for me."

And then Nick and I stood there, our shorts around our knees, our ridiculous little pricks hanging out there for God and the angels to see. Seth had the grace to make at least a token effort to hide his smirk.

"Okay, grab your dicks and get a load of this bitch. Ever seen tits like that?"

I had not, in fact, ever seen tits like that and, as I grabbed my cock, it seconded the motion. As amazing as it now seems, I had never previously attempted to "jerk off," but I took to it like a fish to a frying pan. I would never have imagined I could do anything like this in the presence of other people, but it suddenly seemed as if nothing mattered but the woman on the centerfold and my own swollen dick.

"Hey, easy there, Wanker McGee," Seth said. "This is a dry tugger. Sure, it feels fine now, but you're going to regret that ambition in a minute or two. Slow it down and loosen that grip."

After it was over, Nick and I pulled up our jeans. I felt awful. The experience itself had been great, but immediately followed by a sense of shame and self-loathing. I had just jerked off in the basement of a church in the presence of my best friend and his ne'er-do-well brother. What was wrong with me?

"Welcome to the world of men, you little assholes," Seth said. He tossed the *Playboy* back into the cardboard box. He held out one hand. "Now pay up."

"What do you mean?" I asked. "What do we have to pay for?"

"The lesson, dipshit," Seth said. "You didn't think I'd just offer my services for free, did you?"

"We don't have any money," Nick said.

Seth grinned. "Yes, you do. I just gave each of you a fiver upstairs."

"You said that was our commission," Nick protested. "You can't just take it back."

"It was your commission and you just spent it. Now hand it over."

I briefly considered taking a swing at Seth's smug face, but dismissed the thought. He was too big for me to take by myself and I doubted Nick would attack his own brother. With my eyes rimming red with rage and humiliation and shame, I jammed a hand into my hip pocket and handed over the crumpled five-dollar bill. Nick followed suit.

"Thanks," Seth said. "And by the way, if you tell anyone about me taking the money, I'll let everyone know about both this room and what you two just did. Think about that getting around town." He turned and squeezed his way back through the wall opening and disappeared.

* * *

The disappearance of the money did not go unnoticed by Mrs. Grant, the church treasurer. The next Sunday featured my father delivering disappointed sermons on the evils of graft and greed crafted around appeals for the guilty party to throw themselves on the mercy of God and the church. The congregation was divided into two main factions: one believing it was the random work of some area burglar and the other convinced it was an inside job. Of the latter, most held me as the prime suspect. As the resident atheist, it seemed only logical I would attempt to weaken God's kingdom by stealing from its coffers. No one made this accusation publicly, but I could feel the judgment mounting and more than once caught various members observing me with arched brows and suspicious eyes.

My mother seemed blissfully unaware of the undercurrent of malice toward her errant son and sat through each service with the same beatific smile, nodding in response to her husband's gospel. She did, however, ask me if I had heard anything around town concerning the break-in and robbery.

"Not a thing," I lied, adding to my impressive list of sins.

In order to escape the pressure, I retreated to one of my favorite places: the old shed behind our house. It had a section of flat roof that jutted out from the main structure and caught the sun for a good part of the day, making it perfect for hiding out and reading, especially on Sunday afternoons when Nick was stuck at home. His parents were among those who did not believe in any unnecessary activity on the Lord's Day.

In my hand, I clutched a copy of *Madame Bovary*, trying to convince myself it was anywhere as good as the item in the cardboard box that mocked me from the church basement.

> She clung to Rodolphe. Her eyes, full of tears, flashed like flames beneath a wave; her breast heaved; he had never loved her so much, so that he lost his head and said "What is, it? What do you wish?"
>
> "Take me away," she cried, "carry me off! Oh, I pray you!"
>
> And she threw herself upon his mouth, as if to seize there the unexpected consent if breathed forth in a kiss.

It was pretty good. I could picture the heaving breasts and what might follow the passionate kissing, but it just was not the same. I had heard it said somewhere, probably among a gaggle of sex-starved church ladies, that men were hopeless visual creatures and I was beginning to put quite a bit of stock in this view. Even my potent imagination hit a brick wall when faced with the prospect of competing with those two firm, inviting breasts and swelling thighs . . . I reached down and unzipped my jeans.

A rock hit just over my head. I yelped and scooted to the far side of the roof, desperate to hide both my unzipped jeans and bulging underpants. Shit, what if it was my mother? She was not one to throw rocks, but who knew what she would be capable of if she ever found out what a pathetic little degenerate she was raising.

I eased to the edge of the roof and looked down. Another rock zoomed over my head and ricocheted off the wooden side of the shed, almost hitting me in the face. I ducked instinctively just as another rock, this one small like a pebble, flew in and stung my arm.

"Ow! Who's doing that?"

From behind a stand of brush at the edge of the woods, a head wearing a Detroit Tigers baseball cap rose into view. An arm waved, beckoning me toward the woods. Afraid my mother might have heard my shout, I dropped to the ground and ran, bent over, until safely behind the bushes.

A young girl crouched there. She grinned, her lightly freckled face framed by shoulder-length blonde hair and punctuated by the greenest eyes I had ever seen. Her jeans were rolled up to midcalf and she wore a white t-shirt underneath a patterned pink shirt, which was unbuttoned and knotted at the bottom. Her red sneakers were dirty from the woods and her white, folded over socks still held the remains of a few wild burrs.

"I guess I caught you at something," she said. "What were you doing up there?"

I felt my face redden. "Nothing. It's none of your business."

She grinned. "Oh, you were doing something. At least, you were about to."

"What are *you* doing here? Are you spying on me?"

The girl shrugged. "Not really. If I was worried about being seen, would I have started throwing rocks?"

"Yeah, about that," I said, holding up my arm. It still smarted and was developing a red welt. "I don't think you know your own strength."

"Don't be such a baby." She jerked her hand toward me. "I'm Emily, by the way."

I took her hand and introduced myself. "Do you live around here?"

"We just moved in on the other side of these woods. It's not far. There's a path that runs the whole way."

I knew the area she was talking about. It was exclusive, inhabited by wealthy people and large estates. Nick and I had walked over a few times just to look at the houses, but I had never known anyone who lived there. None of the residents attended Christ's Apostles or sent their kids to my school.

Emily looked at me with her head tilted, as if I were a piece of furniture on a showroom floor and she was appraising my value.

"How old are you?"

"Fifteen."

"Me, too. My birthday is in the fall, though. It used to be kind of a big deal, because it would happen just as school started, but now a lot of the girls think birthdays are dumb. Of course, I don't hang out with most of them anymore, because they are so into makeup and clothes, and think messing around outside is disgusting. My mom says I'll probably never grow up."

"You don't like makeup and clothes? I thought all girls liked that sort of thing."

"They're okay, I guess. You want to see something weird?"

I was taken aback by the sudden change of topic. "What is it?"

"On my way here, I found a snake that tried to eat a bird, but died when the bird's beak stabbed through its stomach. Now they're both dead, just lying by the side of the trail."

"You're making that up."

"If you don't believe me, I'll show you."

I started to call her bluff, but remembered my mother was liable to come looking for me at any time. It certainly would not do to have her find me poking around the woods with a girl. "I can't."

"Why not? Are you scared you'll be sick? It's pretty disgusting."

"I'm not scared." I nodded toward the house. "My mom . . . she'll be calling me for church pretty soon."

"Church? Are you religious?"

"My parents are. I'm an atheist."

"Do they know that?"

"Yeah. I'm their favorite prayer request. I'm something of a celebrity at church."

Emily laughed. "You're funny. What church do you go to?"

"Christ's Apostles."

"Oh," Emily said, raising her chin in recognition. "A neighbor told my parents about that when we first moved in. They said it was pretty far out."

"It is. It's the most conservative church in town."

"Sounds like a scream. I should go with you sometime."

"Do your parents go to church?"

Emily emitted a short laugh. "Ha! Hardly. They pride themselves on being irreligious. My mom likes to say she's spiritual, but I think that just gives her an excuse to be weird. She's really into nature and shit. Are you sure you don't want to go see the snake?"

I shook my head. "Sorry. I have to stay here and wait."

"I should get home anyway," Emily said. "It's probably getting close to dinner time and my mom starts worrying if I don't come home by then. And if my mom gets worried, my dad gets mad. He's kinda like the Hulk. You wouldn't like him when he's angry."

The back door banged open and I looked through the bushes to see my mother walking down the back steps.

Emily started at the noise. "Gotta go!"

I watched her disappear into the woods. She was completely unlike any girl I had met before. She seemed older than her age, but did not seem to have reached the materialism of the older girls I had seen at school, something made even more surprising by the fact her parents were well off. I had to admit she had the development of the older girls. I had not been able to stop myself from looking at her gentle curves, visible even under the loose fitting over shirt.

* * *

Emily started dropping by almost every day. We began spending so much time together that Nick accused me one Sunday of avoiding him.

"Is this because of Seth and what we did in the basement?"

"I'm not avoiding you," I said. "I've just been really busy."

"Busy? What could you possibly be doing? It's fucking summer!"

"Just busy, that's all! Don't be a fucking pest!"

I knew I had hurt his feelings, but spending time with Emily seemed more important. My mother still did not know anything about her. We developed a fake birdcall she used whenever she was waiting in the woods. She asked why the secrecy was necessary and I explained about my parent's belief that fraternization between the sexes was a recipe for lust and the sins of the flesh. I expected Emily to be angry about being kept a secret, but she seemed to enjoy the idea of trysting and did not complain at all when I insisted she never allow herself to be seen from the house.

My mother made bacon and eggs for breakfast. She had always been a good cook, but had spent less and less time in the kitchen over the last couple of years, much to my father's dismay. I remembered when she had spent almost the entire day cooking and baking, and we would have meals like roast beef and green bean casserole or fried chicken and apple pie. Now we were more likely to have a frozen meatloaf dinner. But this Saturday she made bacon and eggs. They were absolutely delicious and I could not help wonder if this was part of a campaign to put me in a good frame of mind for revival. The thought made me feel a little guilty; maybe she was just being nice.

Breakfast was a quiet affair. My mother served up the food, but both parents remained lost in their own thoughts, speaking only to ask for the salt or pepper. After the meal, I helped clean up and my mother retired to her leather chair and picked up her Bible. My father excused himself to his study to prepare for Sunday services.

"Take the bacon grease and dump it in the woods," my mother said, opening the Bible with a finality that suggested she did not wish to be disturbed. "The squirrels and coons love it."

This was also a change. Previously, she would have burst a blood vessel if I had thrown out good grease she could have used for more cooking, but I did as I was told without question, stepping out the back of the house into the warm, late morning sun. I carried the bowl of stinking grease to the edge of the woods and tapped it upside down against a tree trunk. The gelatinous blob of bacon byproduct peeled out of the bowl with a horrible sucking sound that made my stomach twist. It landed, trembling, on a bed of last year's leaves.

"Are you trying to give the animals heart problems?"

I whirled around to see Emily leaning against a tree, arms crossed, smiling. I paused before answering to draw a breath. Why did it seem like she was sneaking up on me all the time?

"You scare easily," Emily said. "Are you always so out of it?"

I shrugged. "I'm just introspective, I guess."

"Introspective, huh? Is that another word for slow?"

"My parents think it is. And I think the animals get enough exercise to be able to eat whatever they want." I hitched up my jeans self-consciously.

"You're probably right. So what are you doing after you dump bacon grease?"

"I hadn't thought about it."

"Want to go swimming?"

"I'm not a very good swimmer."

"You don't have to be good. It's not a contest."

I hesitated.

Emily frowned. "You don't know how to swim, do you?"

"I never learned," I admitted, reddening.

"Your mom never took you to swimming lessons?"

"It wasn't a priority. Swimming is kind of a worldly activity."

"Isn't that why it's fun?"

I did not know how to answer.

As if she sensed my growing discomfort, Emily redirected. "Well, if you don't know how to swim, I'll teach you."

"I don't know," I said. "Where would we swim?"

"You tell me," Emily said. "I'm the new kid around here, remember?"

"There are little lakes and ponds all over, although a lot of them get taken over by tourists this time of year."

"Anywhere private?"

I thought about Mosquito Bay. I had not been there since the incident in April and was not sure I was ready to go back. Then again, this was Emily and I was surprised to find I liked the idea of sharing my special place with her.

"I have a favorite spot hardly anyone knows about," I said. "If you promise to teach me how to swim, I'll show it to you."

"Deal."

A few minutes later an open expanse of water appeared through the trees, a living canvas playing visual staccato between the trunks of oak, maple, and beech trees, and waving orchestral sections of tall, wild grass. We broke through the tree line. Mosquito Bay unfolded before us like the main floor of an enormous concert hall. The gentle waves lapping the rocky shore sounded like applause from an appreciative audience. There was not a tourist to be seen. Not even a fishing boat disturbed the placid surface, to say nothing of the speedboats and Jet Skis that invaded most area lakes during tourist season.

"What lake is this?" Emily asked.

"It's called Mosquito Bay."

"It's awesome! I can't believe how quiet it is!"

"The name might be part of the reason tourists avoid it."

Emily ran straight for the wooden pier jutting into the water. The ancient planks were a weathered mix of brown and gray. It looked like a scab on the skin of a shimmering blue giant. After reaching the pier, Emily turned around and waved to me.

"Hurry up!"

I started forward, but stopped short as I realized I had no swimming trunks.

"What are you waiting for?"

I cupped my hands around my mouth. "I don't have a swim suit!"

To my surprise, Emily grinned. "I don't have mine either!"

I watched in stunned disbelief as she slipped off her shirt and jeans, leaving only a white bra and pair of flowered panties. She gave a single wave and then performed a perfect backflip into the water. I had not moved, but instead stood transfixed to the spot. I did not know what to do. I could run back to the house and get my trunks, but that somehow seemed a betrayal. After all, I had just stood there and watched what amounted to a striptease. And I was not opposed to the idea of jumping into the water after her. Terrified, yes, but not opposed. I decided to hurry to the pier, undress, and get into the water before she surfaced.

My feet had hit only the first plank of the pier when there was a rush of water and Emily's head broke the surface. She was smiling from ear to ear and shaking her head to clear water from her eyes, ears, and nose.

"I thought it would be colder this time of year," she said. Her eyes sparkled and her skin shone in the sun. Her hair was plastered to her head, making it look as if she were wearing the tight swimming cap of an Olympian. "Come on in," she said. "I'll show you how to swim!"

"Don't watch me."

Emily ducked her head and covered her eyes. "Fine, you baby. I'm not looking."

Clumsy with haste and nerves, I shucked off my clothes. In a moment of gratitude, I breathed silent thanks I had thought to put on a fresh pair of underwear that morning. I dropped into the water, holding the side of the pier for safety.

The shock of the water made me gasp.

"I thought you said it wasn't cold!"

"I said I thought it would be colder," Emily corrected. "Start moving around and you'll warm up quick enough."

"How am I supposed to do that? I can't even touch the bottom!"

"Just start moving your legs."

I started churning my legs, causing a wild wake to erupt in the water behind me.

"You don't have to work that hard," Emily said, laughing. "Just kick them forward and back." She moved closer. "Now lean forward and start paddling with your arms."

I tried to follow instructions, but all I could see was me sinking to the bottom of the lake.

Emily laughed. "You're going to have to let go of the pier first."

Against my better judgment, I let go of the rough wooden planks and immediately felt myself slide under the surface of the water. Just like the experience in April, things went quiet. My eyes were open and I could see the mossy sides of the pier supports. Green tendrils waved aimlessly back and forth. Bubbles rose to the surface and I absently wondered if they were coming from me. Was I breathing in water? The water pressed against me. Emily had been right; it seemed much warmer now. I turned my head and saw her treading water just a few feet away. Beneath the surface, I could only see her from the neck down, looking like a decapitated body still kicking. The lake encased her body, the dancing sunspots in the water covering her body like abstract fish scales. She was a headless mermaid, floating in a vast expanse of wet, liquefied gauze. Her underwear lay so near her skin it looked like body paint. I watched, entranced, and did not notice I had stopped kicking and was sinking until a jolt brought me back. I opened my mouth in surprise and took in a great mouthful of water. A gritty geyser of silt cloaked me as my feet sank into the lake bottom. Above, I saw Emily's head appear as she swam straight down. She grabbed my hand and I kicked my feet and, in a moment, we were above the surface of the lake and I was somehow holding onto the side of the pier, gagging on water.

"What the fuck? I told you to paddle!"

"Sorry," I choked. "I . . . I'm . . . not sure what . . . happened."

"You just let go of the pier and sank to the bottom of the lake, that's what happened!" Emily said.

She was yelling at me. Her face was pinched and she was actually angry and yelling.

"Sorry," I repeated.

"Stop apologizing," she said. "Just try it again." She stopped and watched me choke for a moment. "Are you okay?"

I nodded.

"Fine. Then as soon as you get done puking, try it again. And this time, do what I tell you. I'm not going to rescue you next time."

I managed to regain control of myself and began moving my legs forward and back.

"Use your hands like paddles," Emily said. "Like you're in a canoe."

I followed the instructions. My heart was pounding out of my chest, but I gritted my teeth and kept going. Finally, I let go of the pier altogether. Emily bobbed next to me and I felt her arms go under my body.

"Now let go of the pier."

"What if I sink?"

"You're not going to sink, damn it!"

Clumsily, my arms and legs moved. They were not entirely in sync, but I felt as if I were moving forward a little. I looked over at Emily.

"Are you pushing me?"

She shook her head.

"So that means I'm moving? I'm swimming?"

The pissed off look drained from her face. "You're sort of swimming. That's pretty good for a first time, though!"

Without warning, she lowered her hands. I panicked and the surge of fear threw off my tenuous rhythm. A mouthful of lake water finished me off.

"I'm drowning!"

"Oh my god." Emily pushed me back toward the safety of the pier. "Such a baby."

I clung to the pier, regaining my breath. I watched as she moved in the water with ease, at one point flipping onto her back and performing the backstroke in wide circles.

"You're really good at that," I said.

"Thanks. I've been swimming as long as I can remember. My mom told me my dad just dropped me into our pool when I was only one and I started paddling all on my own. I guess it just comes naturally."

"I wish it came naturally to me."

"Are you afraid of water?"

I did not answer right away. I was not sure how to answer, as I was unsure if I was afraid of water or not. Sometimes I thought so, such as whenever my father mentioned baptism. But then there were times when being in the water, more specifically *under* the water, was the only place I wanted to be.

"I'm not sure. Sometimes, I guess."

"It's nothing once you get used to it," she said, speaking with authority. "Before long, you just feel like part of the water."

I nodded. I knew exactly what that felt like.

Emily pointed out toward the middle of the lake. "It looks like there's a tiny island a little ways out. You want to swim to it?"

"I don't think I could make it that far."

"It's not far. Come on, I'll make sure you don't kill yourself."

Emily was right about the distance. It was not far, although it seemed like it at the time. With a combination of my awkward paddling and Emily's support, we managed to limp our way to the island.

The island was really nothing more than an outcropping of rock with a single scraggly tree growing out of one side.

Emily pulled herself out of the water and plopped down on the nearest open spot. I dragged myself out of the water and set about trying to find a place on the craggy knoll that did not include a sharp piece of rock. Emily had found the only such spot as she stretched lazily in apparent luxury. Another cause of my discomfort was the fact we were still clad in nothing but our underwear. I marveled at Emily's level of comfort with her body, watching as she stretched on her back to dry out in the sun. I, on the other hand, sat huddled like a female monkey protecting its young from predators by shielding them between her legs.

Emily sighed and squinted into the bright, light blue sky. "Ever think about the future? Like what you're going to do?"

"The first thing I'm going to do is leave here."

"For where?"

"Anywhere. I've always wanted to see the Upper Peninsula. It's funny that Serenity is so close to the U.P., but still I've never seen it. On the other hand, I might go to a big city, like New York or Chicago."

"What'll you do? Teach swimming lessons?"

"Hilarious. No, I'll write."

"You want to be a writer? What do your parents think of that?"

"They call it a waste of time. They think writers and artistic types are wicked and immoral, and that such a life will lead me down the path to spiritual ruin."

"I think you're already there."

"They're still hoping I'll come around."

The sun, higher in the sky than it had been, was much warmer and I became drowsy, in spite of the inhospitality of the island. I began to relax. There was a strange feeling creeping over the entire scene, something I could only describe as peacefulness. It was a strange sensation, not something I was used to, and I realized just how on guard and tense I was most of the time. These feelings of peace, relaxation, comfort, and even acceptance, were foreign and yet also familiar, like love at first sight.

* * *

Emily's visits stopped after the swimming lesson at Mosquito Bay, although I was unsure why. I doubted it had anything to do with the makeshift swimsuits. She seemed like such a strong and outgoing person that the idea of her staying away out of embarrassment seemed unlikely, although a possibility. Or maybe she thought I was a square or too much of a prude to hang out with. I even entertained the idea she might be angry because I had not tried anything with her. Did she think I disliked her because I had not made a move?

My mother grilled me for a couple of days about my quick departure from the house on the day of the swim. I found it easy enough to lie and say I had been with Nick. He and I had a long-standing agreement to always answer in the affirmative when asked if one had been with the other. It was a great alibi. And, fortunately, my mother seemed too preoccupied to pursue the matter aggressively. Even so, she had a nose for guilt and I must have reeked to high heaven. I finally sought out Nick's company for a little relief. He was grudgingly happy to see me.

"I thought you'd forgotten all about me," he said.

"Of course not. I've just been busy. What, am I your only friend?"

"No, dumbass. It's just been a little boring lately."

"Where's Seth?"

Nick looked at the ground. "He went back to LA."

"When's he coming back?"

"I don't know. Maybe never. He and my parents had a big fight over money, religion, and the fact that Seth doesn't have a 'real job.' So he stormed out and said he'd never be back."

"Wow."

"Yeah. Of course, he's said that before."

"So nothing's really changed, then."

"Not really."

"But you seemed bummed."

Nick shrugged. "Nah. I'm good. What've you been up to?"

Part of my reason for seeking out Nick had been to break the news about Emily, but now it seemed cruel. Seth's departure to LA seemed to be hitting Nick unusually hard. Something was off, but I could not figure out exactly what.

"Aw, not much," I said. "My parents have been keeping me pretty busy around the house."

"Did you hear about the new girl?"

Well, damn it. That is what happened when you lived in a small town. Now Nick had somehow learned my news. Next time, I would not be so careful of his tender feelings.

"Who, Emily?"

"You know her?" Nick's eyes widened and I felt a little better.

"Sure, we've been spending quite a bit of time together. What about her?"

Nick's eyes narrowed. "I thought you were doing stuff for your parents. You've been avoiding me to spend time with a girl, haven't you?"

I was caught and decided nonchalance might be my best tactic. "So what if I have?"

To my surprise, Nick's face broke into a wide grin. "Now that's an excuse I can get behind!" he said, holding up his palm for a high five. "Did you get any pussy?"

Had I gotten any pussy? Was this more Seth-speak?

"Er, no. We did go swimming in our underwear, though." I delivered the news with a coolness befitting James Bond. I almost yawned at the end, but decided that would be going a little too far.

Nick looked like he had been hit by a lightning bolt. "Seriously?"

His reaction was more than I had hoped for, simply delicious, and I felt a laugh of giddy triumph gurgling deep inside.

"You wouldn't shit me, would you?"

"No," I said grandly. "I would not shit you." And suddenly I was laughing great waves of mirth that almost sent me to my knees. Nick looked at me suspiciously.

"Are you lying? Why are you laughing?"

I shook my head. "Not . . . lying," I gasped. "Your face . . . you look like you're about to have a stroke!"

Nick frowned. "You practically skinny dipped with a girl. I haven't had as much as a kick in the ass from one, so excuse me for being a little on the jealous side."

I struggled to pull myself together. "Sorry, sorry."

"So you heard about the girl, right? Emily?"

I suddenly remembered Nick had brought this whole thing up.

I sobered immediately. "What about her?"

"She got caught shoplifting at Dee's."

"The clothing store?"

"Yeah, that one downtown. Next to the diner. We ride past it on the way to get ice cream."

"I know where it is," I said. "What happened?"

"I just told you. She got caught shoplifting."

"Did she get arrested?"

"The cops showed up, but the owner didn't want to press charges. I don't think she wanted to be known as the one who tried to prosecute a kid."

"So what happened to Emily?"

"I'm not sure. I heard her dad was pretty pissed. She's probably grounded or something."

That would certainly explain why she had stopped coming around the house. I had the sudden urge to change the subject.

"So are you looking forward to the revival?"

"Fuck, no," Nick said. "In fact, I can't stop thinking about it. I keep trying to figure some way to get out of it, but other than becoming deathly ill, I can't come up with anything."

"Why are you dreading it so much? Well, besides the obvious fact we'll be stuck in church every night for a week."

Nick looked at the ground again. I had noticed he did this whenever he felt nervous or uncomfortable. "I don't know. I've heard it can be pretty intense. I'm nervous about holding up under the pressure, I guess."

"At least you're not the one everyone thinks stole church money," I said. "I forgot to thank Seth for that, by the way. Now everyone thinks I'm a thief *and* a hopeless denier of Christ."

"Sorry," Nick said. "I never thought Seth would do anything like that. I guess he really needed money. And after my parents turned him down, he didn't have much choice."

"Doesn't he have a job?"

"He's trying to be an actor. But Seth says work is slow in LA right now."

I suspected what was truly at a low ebb was Seth's desire to have a job, but I could tell Nick was feeling shitty, so I kept that thought to myself.

"Maybe you'll feel better once the revival is over," I said, trying to be comforting. "It's only a week."

* * *

"We don't want you hanging around that girl anymore," my mother said.

The words came with a stillness I was not used to from my mother. It was like the proverbial calm before the storm, heavy with intent and judgmentalism. My heart skipped a beat and I held my breath, which caused me to wait just a little too long before asking, "What girl?"

My father huffed. "Don't play dumb. You insult our intelligence and it's disrespectful. You're much too young to be alone with a girl. It has to stop."

I squeezed my eyes shut and forced myself to take another bite of canned beef stew, even though all I wanted to do was run. Of course I knew what girl they were talking about, but could not figure out how they knew. They certainly would have heard about the shoplifting, this being a typically gossip-ridden small town, but that did not connect with me in any way. I risked opening one eye and saw my mother looking down into her bowl of stew, stirring slowly. I noticed she looked older and more tired than usual.

"What girl?" I said.

"That Dunbar girl," she said.

"Who?"

"The girl who was caught shoplifting," my father said. He was losing what little patience he had. "You heard about that, didn't you?"

"Nick told me."

"Well, she was caught shoplifting."

"Right."

"So you'll stay away from now on. She's nothing but trouble."

"How did you—?"

"Know you had been spending time with her?" My father laughed dryly. "Give us a little credit. You can't put anything over on us. And anything we miss, God sees."

"Honey," my mother said, "I know you say you don't believe in Him, but He believes in you." Her eyes welled with tears and her spoon dropped with a clink to the side of her bowl. She reached out with her two hands and gripped mine. Her hands were narrow. The skin was thin and the knuckles seemed oversize. "I'm so worried about you, son."

"You don't have to worry," I said. I wanted to run, run into the woods and never stop running. I had never seen my mother this intense. "I'm fine. Healthy as a horse."

"It's your soul I'm worried about," she said. "If anything were to happen, you'd go straight to hell. Oh God! I can't bear to think about you suffering for eternity!"

I tried to pull my hands away, but her grip was astoundingly firm.

"I know it makes you uncomfortable to see me this way," she said, "but it's only because I love you. I've been carrying such a burden for your lost soul. I can hardly sleep or eat. I'm praying God will send conviction on your soul."

I jerked my hands and they came free. I pushed away from the table. The back of my eyes burned with unshed tears and my stomach churned. I took one more look at my mother, into her reddened, tortured eyes, and ran for the door.

My father's voice thundered behind me. "You can't run from God! He will catch up to you no matter where you go or where you try to hide!"

I did not go far, choosing to climb up onto the shed roof. It was out of sight of the house and I could stay there until I regained my thoughts. The incident had shaken me deeply and I thought about the coming revival with renewed dread. If this was the kind of thing I had to look forward to, maybe Nick was right to be so concerned. At one point, I thought I was going to be sick and hung my head over the side of the roof to gag. Nothing came up, but my stomach felt like I had ingested a gallon of molten lead.

After about an hour, I felt a little better and slid down from my perch. The house was quiet and a furtive peek through the back door showed my mother asleep in her chair with her Bible open on her lap. I felt like I needed to get away from the house and even going to see Nick seemed too close to what had just happened.

The day was firmly in the grip of a heat wave. I could smell it as I shuffled through the leaves, the puffs of dust pooling around my feet, the musty scent of leaves toasting in the Saturday afternoon sun, baking moss, and the sweet aroma of flora rot as nature cycled on, self-cleaning and meticulous. The trees, heavy with leaves, filtered the sun, spattering the ground with a dancing glow, the shafts of light visible in air filled with dust and pollen.

I found the Dunbar lawn immaculate and quiet. Stepping softly, I walked to the side door and peered through the glass, but saw no one. I tried the knob, but it was locked. I walked along the rear of the house, trying to keep a low profile while at the same time appearing harmless. I did not need someone calling the police to report suspicious behavior.

Ahead I saw a white picket fence, its base interspersed with manicured lilac bushes. I heard the splash of water and smelled chlorine. I knelt and pulled the branches aside to peer between the slats of the fence.

Any anxiety I had concerning my immortal soul was entirely forgotten upon sight of gently sloping breasts, damp with sunscreen, gleaming in golden daylight. The rest of the woman's body sparkled with pinprick drops of perspiration. Without warning, my mind flashed back a few years to Sunday School and a portly, middle-aged teacher named Mrs. Grimes who frightened a group of small, impressionable children by telling us God was keeping track of everything we did and one day we would stand before him as he read the list of every bad thing we had ever done.

"Imagine how embarrassed you will feel when all your friends and family hear every bad thing you've ever done or thought," Mrs. Grimes said, just before sending us home with a wag-fingered admonition to be good and pray every night.

I had taken her advice seriously for months, the most miserable and terrifying of my life, before finally weighing possible humiliation against the exhausting work of being perfect and deciding to risk it. Now I knew the entire spiel was nonsense. Even so, I did feel like a complete and utter degenerate as I crouched in the lilacs and peered through the fence. But Satan is remarkably proficient at positive reinforcement and the woman pushed herself up with one long arm, dimpled at the elbow, and reached for a champagne flute on a round, glass-topped table.

The door leading to the pool banged open and I shrank behind the bush. A stocky, powerfully built man strode forward, a piece of creased paper fluttering in his left hand. The woman stiffened.

"Janet!"

She did not answer at first, pausing to take a drink from her glass. "Yes, Frank."

"What the fuck is this!" The man sharply pulled the two ends of the paper, snapping it in her face.

"What is it, dear?"

"A bill, Janet. It's a bill. From that clothing store you're always cooing about."

"Oh yes. I bought a few things. Did I forget to tell you?"

"A few things?" Frank Dunbar waved the paper over his head as if he were a soldier on the front in WWI and the paper was a truce flag. "Did you see the bill? Two thousand dollars! Do you even keep track of what you're spending? Fucking Jesus Christ! You don't even wear clothes most of the time!"

I sat mesmerized by the scene, transfixed by the sight of a man in tan shorts and Hawaiian shirt confronting an exquisitely naked woman who clutched a beverage tightly in one hand. I expected Janet to shrink from Frank's verbal onslaught or at least adopt a somewhat meeker tone, but she surprised me. Perhaps it was the effect of alcohol or the increasing humidity. Whatever it was caused her to pull herself upright, back straight, head back, eyes flashing.

"Consider that my salary, Frank." Her voice sounded gritty. Her teeth were not quite clenched, but her jaw was tight. "You seem to think I work for you, like I'm just another employee, so consider that my wages."

Frank's face twisted and a vein surged, throbbing, on the side of his face and neck. "Damn straight, you work for me. Sometimes I think you only married me for my money and the Dunbar name!"

"And sometimes I think you just married me for my tits!"

Frank leaned forward, towering over the woman. Her will faltered and she flinched. He noticed. Reaching down with one massive hand, he grabbed her crotch and squeezed. Janet cried out, the pain and humiliation evident on a face that crumpled in heartbreak.

"In fact," Frank continued, calmer now that he knew he had won. "You don't just work for me. You belong to me, bitch! You fucking belong to me! I bought you with all the money you spend on clothes and a lifestyle that lets you sit by the pool all day and drink goddamn mimosas!" He released and slapped her with the same hand.

The mimosa fell from Janet Dunbar's hand and smashed on the concrete, the liquid mixing with dust and dirt like the alcoholic tears smearing her mascara.

"Get out, Frank. Just get out." She was not angry any more. Her voice, quiet and threaded with tears, sounded defeated, broken.

The sudden victory seemed to catch Frank off guard. He backed away a step.

"You're going to return that shit." Then he walked quickly inside without a backward glance.

She wilted, looking like a lilac placed too near a flame. She wept without making a sound, the salty water of deep internal pain dropping from unhappy eyes. I wanted to cry with her, but all I could do was sit and watch and hate Frank Dunbar.

* * *

The first revival service put to rest any hopes of an easy week. My father donned the evangelist's mantle with disturbing ease. He drove his points home with violent hand gestures and a high decibel level. As entertaining as the sermon was, I lost focus long before it was over and escaped into the world of the woman on the *Playboy* cover. Even after seeing the centerfold, I was still taken with her, solidly in the grip of first love.

The loud bang of my father's Bible slamming shut yanked me from the reverie. I got ready to stand, but instead of immediately commencing the dismissal prayer, he gripped the sides of the pulpit.

"We are going to have revival," he roared, "whether the Devil likes it or not! We need to stand up and let him know we won't be denied the presence of the Lord. Whoever is committed to renewing the spirit of this church, stand up! The rest of you stay seated. Remember God knows your true heart."

My mother, the dutiful pastor's wife, was the first one to stand, followed closely by every other member in the church. I looked over and saw Nick, that fucking traitor, get to his feet. There was no way he was committed to renewing the spirit of anything, unless it was his own dick. It was good for him there was no God to know his true heart. I felt my mother poking my shoulder, trying to get me to stand, but I resisted until the prayer had finally been said and I was able to make my escape to the basement.

"Holy fuck!" Nick sank to a sitting position with his back to the cinderblock wall. "That was brutal. I thought for sure he was going to give an altar call."

"Yeah. Me, too," I said. "Nice way to sell me out, by the way. So you're committed to renewing the spirit of the church, are you?"

"What did you expect me to do?" Nick said. "Everyone else stood up."

"I didn't."

"Well, I'm not you. I can't pretend like it doesn't bother me to be an outcast at church."

Nick put his head in his hands and, for the first time, I realized how tense he seemed.

"Hey, are you okay? You look terrible."

"I'm kind of freaking out."

"Why, what's going on?"

"I don't know. It's just . . . I don't know. My parents are

constantly on my case."

"About what? What are they on your case about?"

"Religion! After Seth stormed out this last time, I think they realized he was a lost cause, so all their attention has been turned on me. It's like they're terrified of losing another kid to the Devil or something."

"Is that what they said?"

"No, but I don't know what else to make of the fact that my mom keeps coming into my room and pleading with me to get right with God. In the morning, I find Bible verses about salvation and eternity taped to the bathroom mirror. I can't sleep, dude. I'm freaking out! I'm pretty sure I would have gone forward if Reverend Brimstone had given the all-clear."

The idea of Nick going forward subdued any amusement at my father's new nickname. It would mean being alone in my sinfulness and, as convinced as I was this whole salvation idea was a myth, the thought of being even more alone than I already was made my stomach hurt.

"We knew they were going to do this," I said. "This revival is their big chance to convert us. My parents are doing the same kind of stuff."

Nick shook his head in despair. "I don't think I can hold out, man. I know it shouldn't be a surprise, but I didn't think it would be so hard. It's only the first day and I'm already doing stuff I never thought I'd do."

"What do you mean?"

"Nothing."

"What did you do?"

"I'm sorry, man, they got to me."

"Who got to you?"

"Your parents. They came over the other day. Then they and my parents started asking all kinds of questions about us and what we were up to."

"What the fuck did you tell them? Did you tell them about this room?"

"No! Fuck, no! Do you think I'd be down here if I had?"

"You obviously told them something."

"It was that girl. The one who shoplifted."

"You told my parents about Emily?" I never would have guessed Nick would sell me out this way. I struggled to control myself. "What did you say?"

Nick did not answer.

"What the fuck did you say!"

"I just said that you'd been spending time together and that she'd been caught shop—"

Nick's answer was cut off by my fist pounding into his face.

"You piece of shit!" I screamed. "You just told on me to save yourself!"

"Be quiet! Everyone will hear you!"

"Fuck them! I don't give a shit if they do!"

I turned to leave the room and then saw the cardboard box. I stalked over to it, pulled out the *Playboy*, and stuffed it under my shirt.

"And I'm taking this!" I said.

As there was no dignified way to enter or exit the well room, my dramatic departure had to be postponed until I had clambered out. I paused to shout back through the opening to Nick, who still sat slumped against the wall.

"Don't even *think* about telling anyone about this room," I said, "or I'll tell your parents about Seth stealing the money. Think what kind of trouble you'll get into when they find out you knew all about it and didn't tell!"

* * *

As suddenly as she had disappeared, Emily started coming around the house again. She confirmed my original assumption that she had been grounded for shoplifting.

"My dad was pretty pissed," she said. "And you know what happens when he's angry."

"He turns green?"

"Well, that. And he goes a little nuts. I didn't think I'd ever get out of my room." She mumbled something else I did not entirely catch, something like "or him, either," but when I asked what she had said, she pretended she did not know what I was talking about.

The renewed friendship with Emily could not have come at a better time, since revival was in full swing. My father, aka Reverend Brimstone, turned out to be worthy of his new nickname and night after night pounded the local sinners from his perch behind the pulpit. I had never heard so many terrifying tales of hell and lost souls before in my life. He was clearly taking his assumed role as evangelist very seriously indeed.

Every day, I heard my mother in her room and my father in his study, both praying loudly and pointedly for sinners to be saved. Every now and then, one of them would pause and I became convinced they were listening for footsteps to see if I was listening. One day, I tested this theory by walking loudly past my mother's door during her prayer time, making sure the floorboards creaked. She immediately began praying for me by name, asking God to make me sick of sin and so miserable I would not be able to eat or sleep until I had accepted Christ as savior. I tested this theory in turn by going to the kitchen and making a bologna sandwich, which I ate with no difficulty.

Nick folded under the pressure on Wednesday night. My father rose from his chair with unnerving gravity. He walked to the pulpit and dropped his Bible onto it with a thunderous bang. There was a box next to the pulpit, something I had not seen before. It had holes in the side. My father ignored it and leaned over the pulpit to stare intently at his audience.

"God spoke to me today," he intoned, "and told me someone was going to die tonight unless they came to the altar and confessed their sins. He told me this service would be their final chance at salvation. I must ask all the saints here to pray as I deliver the message, that this soul would seize this one last opportunity the Lord has so graciously provided them."

He opened the Bible and read Revelation 20:10 in his booming voice. "And the devil that deceived them was cast into the lake of fire and brimstone, where the beast and the false prophet are, and shall be tormented day and night for ever and ever."

After reading the scripture, he launched into what was his most frightening sermon of the revival. The sermon was mostly comprised of cautionary tales about people who had *almost* made it to heaven, but at the last minute decided to reject Christ. One poor girl, just a teenager, had gone to a camp-meeting service. The altar had been opened for seekers, but she refused to go forward and commit her life to Christ. Friends pled with her, parents wept on their knees, but still, she resisted. At last, they gave up hope and the young girl got in a car with her boyfriend to ride back to town. On the way, they were hit by a drunk driver. The young girl was killed instantly, decapitated as her head crashed through the windshield.

"One minute, she was having a 'good time' with her sinful boyfriend and the next, she was up to her neck in the flames of hell!" my father thundered. He had worked himself into a frenzy. His face was contorted and sweat gleamed on his forehead and ran down the side of his corpulent face. A white fleck of spittle sat lodged in the corner of his mouth. He paced the platform like a caged lion waiting to be released into the coliseum. "This is not just a story to scare you to God, this is a warning from God himself! Hell is real, Hell is real, Hell is real!" As he repeated the phrase, he pounded the pulpit. "Come to God, sinners, before it's too late! Don't let your foolish pride send you to a place of eternal agony!" He reached down and picked up the box and set it on top of the pulpit. He ripped open one flap and reached inside. He grappled with something and then, with a flourish, brought out a long, black, writhing snake that hissed and twisted. "This snake is deadly poisonous," my father bellowed. "Watch as it bites my hand!" He waved his bare hand before the snake, which responded by striking forward and burying its fangs into the soft flesh between thumb and forefinger. "Poison courses through my veins and yet I stand unaffected," my father said. "Now if you don't believe that is God, may he have mercy on your soul!"

In response to some unseen signal, the organist moved to her instrument and began playing "Just as I Am" in a low, moving fashion. The audience at first had been shocked by the sight of the snake, but the sheer emotion and electricity of the atmosphere quickly made them forget their fear. They entered into the spirit with great shouts and waving of hands. One older man broke from his place and began running down the aisles like someone half his age.

I risked a glance at Nick and saw his parents urging him out of the pew. His dad had one arm around Nick's shoulder and his mom stood in the aisle, weeping, beckoning him to follow. As I watched, Nick's face crumpled and he started crying like a baby. Big tears rolled down his face. He half ran, half stumbled out of the pew and down toward the altar. He almost fell over it and as he knelt, the entire church erupted in a chorus of hallelujahs and praise the Lords.

I was fucked.

My mother was even quieter after Nick's conversion. I knew she was disappointed I had not followed Nick's example and suspected she also resented being left out of the post-altar call celebration. How she would have loved to have been the mother of the church's newest Christian! I thought briefly that perhaps I was being too hard on her, but decided I did not care. I had been frighteningly close to caving that night and was beginning to wonder if I would be able to hold out. It was not just the fear of hell, which was actually quite real during the services, but was also the intense peer pressure and the constant judgment. And it was something I could not escape. It was not as if I could simply choose not to go to the services, something I would have done in a heartbeat. *Your next heartbeat might be your last,* as my father said.

There was also a growing sense of guilt associated with living with my parents. I knew I was a disappointment to them. Aside from all their faults, they had provided me with food, shelter, and education. And I could not give them the one thing they truly wanted: my own confession of belief. It weighed heavier on me than I cared to admit and would be the main reason for going up front to the altar. Outside of church, I was not all that concerned about my soul. It was easy to be an atheist outside in the bright sunshine, a cool breeze against my face. But inside a church sanctuary, hot and stuffy with emotional, hysterical people, your heart pounding and your mouth dry like sand, listening to the ranting of a gifted orator, it was a different matter altogether. That was when the years of training and indoctrination kicked in and threatened to muzzle even the clearest mind.

* * *

The next morning I awoke to an empty house and a note from

my mother that said she had gone to the grocery store and that my father would be at the church until after noon. It had rained all night, but was now letting up, even though the sky was still heavy and gray. I threw on jeans and a t-shirt and was about to settle in with a book when the telephone rang.

"Hello?"

There was silence and then an odd sound, like someone choking or swallowing hard.

A voice, wavering and strained, said my name once.

"Hello? Who is this?"

The line went dead. It had sounded like Emily's voice, although I could not be sure. I hurried to the door, shoved my feet into sneakers, and ran to my bike.

It started raining again on the way to Emily's house, but I was almost there, so I kept going. I had a nagging feeling I should have called 911, but what would I have told them? That I had gotten a hang-up phone call? That I had a feeling something bad had happened?

I found Emily sitting on the front steps. She looked as though she had been waiting for me. She wore the Tigers baseball cap from the first time I had seen her, with shorts and a t-shirt. Her hair hung wet and she sat with her hands clasped around bare knees.

I waved and leaned my bike against a tree. She did not wave back. A feeling of dread fell over me like a heavy blanket and my heart thudded in my chest. I walked over to her, my feet squishing on wet grass.

"Hi," I said.

She did not answer, did not even look at me. She did not seem to be looking at anything, just staring into empty space with wide, unblinking eyes.

"Emily? Are you okay?" I sat down on the steps next to her

and touched her shoulder. It was like touching a corpse. "Emily? What's the matter? Talk to me." Panic rose in my gut.

Without speaking, she got up and began walking around the side of the house. I followed on wooden legs and when I saw she was headed for the pool, I knew what had happened.

The rain pelted the pool surface. The tiny droplets were mesmerizing as they turned the water into a liquid pincushion. Janet Dunbar floated face down in the middle of the pool, her hair spread around her head like a child's drawing of a sunrise. Her naked body bobbed gently and I saw that her wrists and fingers hung heavy with rings and bracelets. I stared into the pool. I knew I should say something, do something, but could not function. It was Emily who finally spoke.

"I found her like this. I think she's been in there all night."

"Have you called anyone?"

"Just you."

"How long have you been sitting out here?"

"I don't know." She started shivering.

"Maybe we should go inside and wait. I'll call for help."

"I don't need to go inside."

"But maybe you—"

"I don't need to fucking go inside! Jesus! Just call whoever the fuck you think is going to be able to help!"

The blaring siren somehow took us by surprise.

Sheriff Tolliver and a deputy walked into the pool enclosure. The deputy looked concerned; Tolliver looked like he always did, as if he had a stick up his ass.

They stood on the edge of the pool, just looking.

The deputy removed his hat.

Sheriff Tolliver said, "Must have fallen in last night. Sleep walking, a little too much to drink. A clear accident."

"Could've been a suicide," the deputy said.

"Not a chance," Tolliver said. "People hardly ever commit suicide by drowning, despite what the movies would have you believe. Drowning is almost always accidental. It's just too terrifying. Once the brain starts losing oxygen the only thing the victim can think about is staying alive. That's why whenever someone *does* drown on purpose they have to first swim out so far that they couldn't save themselves if they tried." He bent on one knee and peered at the body. "Somebody told the husband yet?"

They both looked at Emily.

"I don't know where he is," she said.

"Well, don't worry," Tolliver said. "We'll track him down. Do you have any family in the area?"

Emily shook her head. "We just moved here."

"I'll take you on down to the station, then, until we can contact your dad."

An ambulance pulled up and two paramedics jumped out. They grabbed a stretcher from the back and ran toward the pool.

"She's dead, people!" Tolliver called out. "Don't give yourselves a stroke."

The paramedics slowed their pace, but looked at each other, their dislike of the sheriff apparent on their faces. They set up the stretcher and prepared to retrieve the body.

Tolliver looked over at me. "The girl probably shouldn't see this."

I pulled at Emily's arm, but she refused to move. She was a statue, her face smooth and hard like marble.

"You've seen enough," I said. "I know you're tough enough to handle it, but you've seen enough."

"Fuck you. God . . . I can't believe she killed herself. I mean, I can, but I can't."

"It might have been an accident. You heard what the sheriff

said."

"Fuck the sheriff!"

I looked over at Sheriff Tolliver, but he was busy giving superfluous orders.

"My mom never swam at night," Emily said. "Her main reason for using the pool was to stay tanned. And she never wore that much jewelry all at once. Besides, she probably would have been too drunk to climb back out of the pool once she was in. Maybe she *did* change her mind and try to save herself afterward."

For the first time since I had arrived, I saw a twinge of real grief cross Emily's face.

It took both paramedics to pull Janet Dunbar from the pool.

"It's as if the water don't want to let her go," one said.

I watched them load the woman onto the stretcher, her body dripping with water and jewelry. Although the body was too recently dead to have changed much, it was still the worst thing I had ever seen. I wanted to throw up.

The second paramedic whistled long and low at the sight of the jewelry. "Maybe all the commercials are wrong," he said. "Maybe diamonds don't make women happy."

Her eyes were open, large, confused. The weight of the tragedy hit me like an incoming wave on Lake Michigan crashing into a sandcastle, and I felt my insides crumble. Water ran from her hair, pooled in the corners of her eyes and then ran down like an endless stream of tears. I wanted to cry with her, but all I could do was stand and watch and hate Frank Dunbar.

* * *

As the final revival service approached, the pressure mounted. The tension at home was thick enough to choke on. I could feel my resolve weakening. My mind had not changed, my heart had not changed, but the idea of playing the part of a reformed sinner was growing more appealing. My mother's praying increased in both frequency and volume. My father retreated into sullen anger. I began to suspect the revival had been concocted entirely with me in mind. I could not forget my mother's tortured face as she pleaded for my salvation. What harm would it do to play the part? It would make a lot of people happy. It would make for a lonely existence, at least until I was old enough to leave home, but things could not get much lonelier than they already were. Nick was gone from my life; as an unrepentant heathen I was off limits to him. I had not heard from Emily since that awful day. I had ridden my bike to the Dunbar residence, but it had been deserted. No signs of life and no answer when I rang the bell. The newspaper ran an article that said the funeral would be held in Janet Dunbar's home state of Florida. I assumed Emily and her dad would return, but had no idea when. Or if she would ever feel like hanging out again. I was sure I would not. Janet Dunbar's death had affected me much more deeply than I thought it would, plunging me into a state of melancholia. My parents assumed God was using the traumatic event to draw me unto himself. I would not go so far as to say they were happy the death had occurred, but they would shed no tears if it pushed me closer to salvation. I was emotionally exhausted and teetered on the edge of capitulation. I was tired of fighting.

    I sat in my room reading *The Sun Also Rises* by Hemingway when I heard my mother close the bathroom door and turn on the bathtub. Soon after, the moans began. They were low at first, barely audible, then built upon themselves. My mother was praying ahead of that night's service. The moaning periodically dissolved into sobbing before beginning all over again. It had become a regular occurrence, but this time they were louder, more wrenching, more piercing. The moans increased until they were screams and then shrieks. I sat upright on the bed, eyes wide open, book falling from limp fingers as I listened in horror. This was a sound I had never heard before. Then I heard a crash from the bathroom and I was at the door before I knew I was moving. I burst into the bathroom.

"Mom!"

She sat in the tub, naked, rocking forward and back.

"It's blood," she whispered. "There's so much blood."

The shower curtain had fallen to the cold bathroom tiles like a torn veil, the rod torn from wall brackets. She held a Bible in her hands and I watched as she tore the pages out one by one and dropped them into the water. The tub faucet was still running, the room filled with the roar of rushing water. But the thing I saw most clearly were the bruises.

* * *

As I look back, the final revival service is a faded memory. Like an old impressionist painting, it lacks specific detail, but is rich in emotion and implication. I do not remember what my father preached or what songs were sung. I remember how I felt.

The room was hot, I was sweating, my heart was pounding. The stale air was thick and full of noise and rank. People were shouting, but I could not hear individual words; it was just a cacophony of moans and wails and shouts. I was standing, brought to my feet by rough, grasping hands under my arms and on my collar, pushed and carried through a crushing throng of pressing humanity—hot and sweating, heavy and dark—moving inexorably forward. I saw my father—his face was a mass of lines and dripping flesh, twisted, but indefinite. His eyes—I remember his eyes—black and burning—his mouth opened: "Bring him! Bring him to the altar!" Strong hands pulled me, shoved me. I planted my feet.

My shoes skidded and bumped along the carpeted aisle. The swell of the organ above the fray. The altar approached, the press of people moved closer. My knees gave out and I felt myself falling.

I remember even less after that: my hands planted, palm down, on the varnished wood of the altar; pushing myself upright; standing, turning; lashing out with a clenched fist at the nearest face, one unrecognizable in its fervor—was it Nick? I kicked and screamed and punched my way to the door. Gradually, the mass gave way before me. I hit the door with my shoulder and fell onto the concrete steps in front of the church. The air was cool after being inside and I drew it into my lungs like a drug. And I knew I was leaving this place. I would be what I wanted to be, I would write what I wanted to write, and I would not return until I had become successful enough to show them all how small and petty their lives really were.

Part Three

Ever since I agreed to write Nigel Moon's final novel, he and I had been spending a good deal of time together. It was to be expected, given the fact I was writing a book that would have his name on it, but the strange thing was, he rarely asked about the book's progress. We talked about many things, often writing, but hardly ever anything specific concerning the project. At first I felt it to be the elephant in the room and volunteered information. He would act disinterested and change the subject. Eventually I stopped giving him updates and satisfied myself with drinking alcohol at the Jesuit and discussing life with my benefactor.

The truth was the writing was going quite well. Moon had been correct; having the pressure of my unstable economic condition off my shoulders proved to be immensely helpful in focusing on the task at hand. Not having to write for money freed my mind and allowed me to tap into the inner creativity I could not previously afford. I fell into a routine. I would get up at nine o'clock and shower. Then I would sit down and write until noon, at which time I would migrate to the Jesuit for lunch and drinks. Often Moon would arrive around the time I was done eating. He would sit down at his booth and order a sandwich. I would order a drink and by the time I finished drinking, he was done eating. I would then join him at his booth and we would talk for an hour or two about whatever happened to be on his mind. We never ate together.

Today I watched as he finished his usual, a turkey sandwich on rye, and settled back with the rest of his Pabst. I walked over and slid into the booth. He looked up at me and began talking without preamble.

"The reason people are unhappy is because they have unreasonable expectations." The hunting cap with the red flannel pattern was pulled down and hid his eyes. "I lived my life expecting nothing. And when I expected something, I expected it to be bad."

"And was it?"

"Not usually."

"So you have spent your entire life waiting for bad things to happen? That seems like a waste."

Moon sat a little straighter. "I didn't wait for bad things to happen. I lived my life, that's what. I did whatever I wanted, whenever I wanted."

"You sound as if you wanted bad things to happen."

"Don't be a fool. Nobody likes bad things. You don't like bad things. I don't like bad things. But you know what I hate more than bad things?"

He waited, but I had no response. So I waited and drank and he finally gave up.

"You know what I hate more than bad things? Being disappointed. That's what. Take it from me. If you always expect the worst, you'll be pleasantly surprised a lot of the time. If you always go around being a fool optimist, you'll spend your life being upset because things didn't go the way you expected. You'll think life is unfair. That you're somehow being treated poorly."

"I have always heard that life is not fair."

"Life isn't fair or unfair, boy. Life just is."

"That is depressing."

"You shitting me? That's the most liberating thing I can think of."

"I may be too drunk to follow you."

Moon sighed and leaned forward. The yellowish light of the bar sallowed his craggy face. "I don't think you're drunk enough, boy. You still have a wall up in your head. Think about it. The world is full of unhappy people. They kill themselves by the thousands and I'm not talking about the terminally ill. For God's sake, I'll pull my own plug if I get that far gone. I'm talking about people who thought life would be one way and it ended up being another. It may not even be bad. It's just different. So they hate it."

"There must be more to it."

"Think about this: what if no one had any expectations?"

"Well, for one thing, nothing would get done."

"Bullshit."

Emboldened by the whiskey, I pressed my point. "Without expectations we wouldn't have any technological advancements, no cures for disease, no giant leaps for mankind."

"No war, no poverty, no sadness—"

"You are losing me again."

"What's sadness, boy?"

"The absence of happiness?"

"Wrong. Lack of fulfilled expectations. Give me an example of a sad person."

I sat back and remembered a friend who was jilted at the altar and spent the next six months in therapy with suicidal tendencies. I shared the story.

"And why was your friend disappointed?"

"Because she was left at the altar."

"No. She wanted to get married and expected that to happen."

"She was engaged."

"Not relevant."

"It seems like a reasonable expectation to me."

"Her expectations let her down. That's the point. Try to keep up, boy."

"Okay, then how about this: somebody's loved one has an incurable disease and they die. Are you saying the person left behind does not have the right to be sad?"

"Never said they don't have the right to be sad. Never said it was possible to avoid all sadness. I said the reason people are so unhappy is because they have unreasonable expectations. They go through life thinking they'll be the exception to life's rules. Especially the one that says things are going to happen that we don't like. This country is mired in materialism. We have more opportunity than anywhere on earth. Yet we are one of the most miserable countries. Why is that?"

"Reality television?"

He guffawed. "That's more a symptom than cause. No. It's because Americans are taught from a young age that we have certain inalienable rights. That we are owed certain things and should expect a certain standard of living. If you tell someone from the moment they can understand that they are special and should only expect the best from life, you can't be surprised if they feel like crap after finding out they aren't unique and will have to settle for second, third, or fourth in almost everything."

"People are going to be sad. That is just the way it is."

"Of course. You can't escape it. But we're not dealing with just a little melancholy. We're facing an epidemic of depression."

"And you think it is caused by expecting good things to happen?"

"I think it's exacerbated by the tendency of our society to think we're owed good things. We're not owed anything. You can't help being affected by things out of your control. But you don't have to give those things the power to control your life. And that's what happens when you set up a bunch of glowing expectations."

I drained my drink. "You are a terrible person and I do not want to talk to you anymore."

He laughed again. "It's just as well. Don't you have a book to write?"

* * *

"Would you like some more wine?" Kate peered over the rim of her glass.

This had also become part of my routine: spending the early evening with Kate. Dinner, a movie, cuddling, sex, and then back to my hotel room for more writing. It was a comfortable existence. It was also completely different from my ritual. In fact, none of the old ritual existed. Even the writing was different. But somehow I accepted the change with little to no reservation, something I never thought I would be able to do. I rarely thought about it, and felt no sense of loss.

I accepted the wine and looked into her blue eyes. They crinkled at the edges as she smiled, her lips red through the glass, stained with Cabernet Sauvignon. In the background, Michael Bublé sang "Cry Me a River." I sipped the wine and then set the glass on the table. I took Kate in my arms.

"You make me happy, Kate. And I have not felt happy since . . . well, I am not sure when I was last happy."

"You make me happy, too," she said. "It's so strange, us being thrown together like this."

"Thrown together?"

"I just mean the way we met. So random."

"We were in the right place at the right time. That would be a first for me."

"You have a thing for bad luck?"

"I have a thing for bad decisions."

She raised her glass. "Then let's toast to good choices, shall we? Maybe you've turned a corner."

I retrieved my wine and our glasses clinked together. "I think maybe I have."

I wrote late that night. The story swept me away and the words flowed so easily I was afraid to turn off the faucet for fear I would not be able to get it started again. And so I just continued to write. The word count in the lower right of my screen churned faster than the national debt clock and I felt the precious sense of creative adrenaline I craved.

When I checked the time, it was almost 2:00 a.m. I sat back, stretched. My neck popped and when I stood up, my legs ached in protest. My fingers were sore and my shoulders burned. I walked to the window for a quick breath of air. I pushed the window up a crack and then closed it just as quickly. It was well below freezing. The cold air revitalized my system.

I began to turn from the window, but caught a glimpse of a shadow moving near the lake. I could just make out a human figure. I watched with interest as it walked haltingly forward, occasionally stopping to look over the water before continuing on. At one point it appeared to stumble or lose balance. I held my breath as it teetered near the water's edge. Something was not right. Not many people chose to stroll the lakeshore during a winter night and this particular person did not appear to be in complete control of their faculties. I squinted, trying to make out more detail. There was something familiar about the form. I was not the hero type. I generally believed people should get themselves out of whatever messes they got into, but for some reason, perhaps the familiarity of the figure, I grabbed my coat and ran down the stairs to the parking lot. I hurried around the corner of the hotel, slipping a little on the ice, and headed for the lakeshore. I looked for the figure, but could see nothing. Then I saw it, moving away down the lake path. It bent low inside a heavy coat, head down, feet shuffling. I moved to catch up, but my foot hit a patch of ice hidden under fresh snow and I fell hard onto concrete. I caught myself with the point of my chin. My vision tunneled. I might have blacked out for a minute or maybe it simply took me longer to get to my feet than I thought. In either case, by the time I stood up the figure was nowhere to be seen. I let out a string of highly creative profanities and grabbed a handful of snow to press against my chin. It was bleeding profusely, but with a little luck I might be able to avoid stitches. There was nothing like a cut on the chin for bleeding.

* * *

"What happened to your chin?" Moon asked.

"Slipped on the ice." I related the story from the night before.

Moon looked thoughtful. "Funny, it seems like I've heard that before."

"Déjà vu?"

"All over again. I once knew a guy who thought déjà vu was composed of memories from a past life. He said he went south—to Florida, I think—just visiting. Some friends were trying to drive him to some historical location and even though he had never been there, never even been to Florida, he was able to direct them straight to it."

"GPS?"

"He claimed he had memories from a previous existence."

"Did he also have some prime Floridian real estate he wanted to sell you?"

"I didn't say I believed him. I just said that's what he told me."

"It is fun to think about, I suppose. Do you think you slipped and fell on the ice in a previous life?"

I was joking, but Moon took the question seriously.

"No, it isn't that," he said. "I just feel like I knew that story somehow."

"Did you happen to be out walking the lakeshore last night?"

Again I was joking and again Moon took the question at face value.

"Can't say I was. Pretty cold out last night."

"Indeed," I said. "I would like to track this phantom down just to tell him off for making me freeze my nuts off."

"How's the book coming?"

The question, so unexpected and overdue, took me completely by surprise.

"Oh, the book is . . . coming along just fine, actually."

"Good. I got a call from the publisher. They're anxious to move this process along."

"I am writing as quickly as I can."

"Not trying to pressure you. I just need a blurb, a bone to throw to the suits."

"I might be able to have a rough draft in a few weeks, if the writing goes as it has been."

The timeline seemed to satisfy him and he finished his Pabst without mentioning the book again.

"How's the book coming?"

I turned toward Kate. She was tossing a salad and wearing a V-neck sweater that hugged the contours of her body. Her red hair was pulled back loosely and fastened at the nape of her neck with an ivory clasp.

"What makes you ask that?"

She shrugged and a bra strap slipped into view. "I don't know. Just asking, I guess. You don't have to talk about it if you don't want to."

"It is just that you are the second person today who has mentioned it."

"Really? Who else?"

"The old guy whose book it actually is."

"I guess he has a right to know."

"Yes. But he has pointedly avoided talking about it until now."

"Maybe something has changed."

"He said he was getting questions from his publisher."

"You don't believe him?"

"I am not sure. I suppose there is no reason not to."

"So why question it?"

"I have no idea. Maybe I just resent feeling pressured."

"I'm sure he was just checking in."

"Maybe." I moved behind her and kissed her earlobe. "Ready for me to pour the wine?"

* * *

In a departure from my schedule, partly as a result of the new writing timeline I had recklessly given Moon, I continued keeping late hours, though it became more of a struggle than it had been that one blissful night. I spent a lot of time either making and drinking coffee or observing my computer screen as if it were the portal to an alien dimension. Even so, I made respectable progress and felt mildly accomplished each time I closed the laptop.

This particular night I had at least written enough to be able to sleep, assuming my ill-advised coffee consumption did not require too many trips to the bathroom. As I stood up from the desk, my gaze drifted out the window as it always did. During breaks in the nighttime cloud cover, which seemed all too rare, the moonlight shone and sparkled on the icy lake. It was not completely frozen over and fragments of ice amid the moving water created a blue-black tableau of languid, heartbreaking motion. So lovely it provoked a sense of nostalgia for things not experienced and places not visited. The snow banks along the shore glistened and sparked to Debussy's *Clair de Lune*, because this was the kind of scene that made one hear it.

And then I heard a discordant note: a lone figure moving haltingly along the snowy, icy path, just as it had the other night. It stopped once and looked around slowly, then continued walking. Something else caught my eye. Another figure, smaller, thinner, moving faster, trying to catch up to the first. I opened the window just a crack. On a still cold night, sound traveled well and I might have been able to hear voices. But nobody spoke and I closed the window against the chill. The smaller figure closed the distance and put a hand on the shoulder of the first. It stopped and turned suddenly, backed away. The second figure appeared to plead, pointing back where it had come from. After several minutes, the first relented and allowed itself to be led back down the path.

"Must be some old guy off his nut," I said aloud as I fell into bed. "Poor bastard."

* * *

"There's no such thing as free will," Moon said. He sipped his Pabst.

"Never?"

"Never. We have no choice in the roads we take. We like to think we're in control, but we are following a prescribed path, an ancient way. Every misstep, every triumph, every success, every failure—they are all part of the plan, landmarks on the journey."

"You are getting a little into the deep end for me."

"Over your head?"

"Oversold. You are asking me to believe anything anyone ever does is because they had no choice."

"So you *do* get it. Maybe you're not as dumb as you look."

"I get what you are saying, not that I believe it."

"Acceptance is not the same as belief, boy."

"Neither do I accept it."

"Every experience changes us a little," Moon said. "Sometimes a lot. They make us the people we are. Every experience molds our humanity, our spirit."

"I can generally agree, but that is much different than saying every experience had to be experienced."

"Well, it did in order to make you who you are today. If your past experiences, even one of them, had been different, you'd be a different person. Perhaps only slightly different, but different."

"That still does not mean they all *had* to happen," I said. I sipped my Johnnie Walker Black, which did not taste quite as good now that I could afford it. "Of course there have been things in life beyond my control. For example, into which family I was born. But there are a lot of other things—what college I attended, what make of car I purchased, whom I dated—that were, at least in some capacity, under my direct control."

"That's easy to say now. But all you really know is you made the choices you made. The only way to know if you had an option would be to go back in time and choose differently."

"So this is all just an exercise in futility."

"It's academic, I suppose."

"Precisely." I turned toward the bar and caught Archer's eye. He ambled over.

"Another Johnnie?"

"No, actually," I said. "I'll take a Pabst."

"Really. You want a Pabst?"

"It is for a good cause."

"Whatever you say." Archer moved off in the manner of a man fetching a gun for a suicidal friend to whom he is close.

"You look horribly pleased with yourself," Moon said. "I gather you think you're making some clever point with this little charade?"

"Just wait."

Archer returned with the beer. I drank liberally, then set the glass down and grimaced.

"There. I hate Pabst. Both you and Archer know it. Yet I chose to order and drink it. I exercised free will in opposition to what I really wanted."

"And you feel this disproves my earlier point?" Moon said.

"Yes."

"Cute. But you really only illustrate what I just said. The only way to know if you could have avoided ordering that particular drink would be to rewind time and do things differently."

I sighed. "Why must you torture me with these faux philosophical ramblings of yours?"

"I have no choice," Moon said, looking clever. "It's part of my life's path."

I groaned.

"And also because you're the only one who will sit and listen to them," he finished. He motioned toward my half-empty glass of Pabst. "You going to drink that?"

"Hell, no."

He reached over and took it.

"What about criminals?" I said.

"What *about* criminals."

"Do they not have a choice in their nefarious deeds? I am not talking about the person who speeds, smokes a little weed, or overstays their welcome at a parking meter. What about murder, rape, molestation . . . do you really mean to tell me they have no choice?" I expected him to back away and create an exception to his own rule. Instead, he nodded.

"Yes, I do."

"I am not sure how I feel about that."

"How so?"

"It feels like you are taking the side of those whom most people would say need to be locked away for the good of the public."

"I never said our actions don't have consequences. Just that they are unavoidable."

"I think you would have a hard time selling this to a jury. 'Your honor, my client could not help murdering the little old lady and fucking her corpse. He was simply following his path.'"

"Fate is not a defense. Society has a responsibility to protect itself, certainly."

"But does it not seem cruel to punish people for pursuing decisions they had no choice in making?"

"You're making the mistake of believing, or at least wanting to believe, that life—existence—should be kind and gentle. Or even fair. Think about the criminally insane, those who endanger society. We confine them as criminals, yet they had no choice in their actions. They behave as would anyone with that particular mental affliction."

"A different matter."

"Is it? We're no further along than the criminally insane when it comes to understanding our place in the universe. We're like babies flailing in a crib and thinking we make the world spin. We know nothing."

"Your philosophy is fucked," I said, sliding from the booth. "At first glance it seems sympathetic and warm, but on closer inspection it becomes quite ugly."

"Life is ugly," Moon said. "That's why it's so beautiful. And take this with you: if we have no choice, then we are all doing our best. And how much easier is it to practice kindness on ourselves and others if we know we are all doing our best?"

* * *

"He sounds like quite the philosopher, this writer friend of yours," Kate said. We had begun binge-watching a popular show on Netflix and as she got the show ready to play I had given her a summary of my earlier conversation with Nigel Moon.

"He fancies himself one," I said. "Mostly he just rehashes old ideas and pretends he came up with them."

"That seems harmless enough."

"Harmless, but annoying."

Kate smiled and started the program. We watched for fifteen minutes and then I looked over to see she had fallen asleep and was lightly snoring. I paused the show and shook her shoulder. She awoke with a start.

"What's wrong?"

"Nothing. You fell asleep."

"No, I didn't."

"Yes, you did. You were snoring."

"Sorry. I'm just a little tired tonight."

"Are you all right?"

"Just tired. I worked late last night." She pushed up from the couch. "If it's okay, I think I'll head home. Maybe we can pick this up tomorrow?"

"Sure, no problem," I said. "Go ahead. I will clean up."

"Sorry to leave you with a mess."

I closed and locked the door behind her. I went to the window and held up the blind to watch as she crossed the parking lot to her car. Her slim form inside the winter coat, the now familiar gait . . . the second dark form from the other night. It had looked and moved exactly as Kate did now, the movements and posture the same. I let the blind fall back into place and went to the bedroom. From there I could see the lake, the snowy path, the drifts. I replayed the earlier night's scene. It had been Kate. I could see her, just as before, moving quickly to reach the first dark figure, entreating, convincing.

* * *

The next morning I went early to the Jesuit. It was empty except for Archer, who leaned against the counter, wiping glasses and watching CNN. I sat on a stool and pressed my forearms against the polished mahogany of the bar. The place was different when deserted. Quieter, obviously, but more eerie than peaceful. Like an empty church. Archer pulled his attention from the wall-mounted television.

"You're early."

"I woke up early. It ruined my routine."

"You and your routine. Moon has one, too. Must be a writer thing."

"Is it too early for a drink?"

"Judgmental folk shouldn't own bars. The usual?"

I nodded. I watched him pour the whiskey.

"Tell me something, Archer," I said. "Earlier you said information about Moon was 'privileged.' What did you mean by that?"

Archer set the glass down in front of me. "Things haven't changed." He looked up, but kept his head lowered. "You hear something?"

"I saw something. At least, I think I did."

"Whatever it was, it's probably best to forget it."

"I do not think that will be possible."

Archer picked up the remote and muted the television. "I can see you're going to tell me something I don't want to hear."

"But maybe it is something I should hear."

Archer dropped the remote onto the bar. "Fine. What did you see?"

I told him the story of the dark figures in the night.

"And you think this girl, Kate, was one of them?"

"I am sure of it."

"So who was the other one?"

"I . . . I keep thinking it was Moon. But that would mean Kate and Moon know each other and she has never mentioned that. In fact, she has always acted as if she has never heard of him, even though she is incredibly well read."

"You hadn't read him."

"What are you not telling me, Archer?"

He sighed. "You're being a real pain in the ass. And putting me in a very awkward situation."

"I have a lot to lose if something is off with that guy," I said. "I realize you are friends with him, but we are friends as well."

Archer poured himself a quick drink. "Shit. You're in business with him, so I guess you have a right to know."

"Know what?"

"Moon . . . has a mental condition. Dementia or something. Started a year or two ago and has gotten worse since then. Causes him to hallucinate, forget who he is, go somewhere and not know how he got there, become lost and confused—"

"My god," I said. "When was someone going to tell me?"

"It's not really about you, son. The man's sick."

"The hell it is not about me. I am supposed to be writing his book!" I paused. "Wait, is this why he wanted me to write it in the first place?"

Archer nodded.

"So that entire tale about being burned out was a myth."

"Not entirely. It's just that the dementia is largely what caused the burn out. He'd gotten to where he couldn't focus enough to write, couldn't get the words on the page somehow. He'd spend hours typing only to read it over later and find it was all just a bunch of unconnected gibberish. The last couple of his books had to be so edited that they came out sounding nothing like the other books. And certainly nothing like that early one you read."

"What does his publisher think?"

"As far as I know they're in the dark. He hired his own editor the last couple of times. But this time he couldn't even give the editor anything to work on."

"And that is where I came in."

Archer nodded. "And mighty timely it was."

"For Moon, you mean."

"For both of you. Don't pretend like you didn't need the work."

"I hate the deception."

"You've never done something in a time of desperation? Bent the rules? Played it under the table? The man is at the end of not only his career, but his life. I'm not saying it was right to keep it from you, but perhaps as a writer you can see why he did it."

"Do you know the girl?"

"Girl?"

"Kate."

"She's his granddaughter."

"Oh my god."

"It doesn't look good, I'll grant you. But try not to jump to conclusions."

My feet hit the floor as I slid from the stool. My hands shook, but I managed to grab the glass of Walker and hurl it against the wall. "Fuck you, Archer. Fuck you all. No conclusions need to be jumped to. It is perfectly obvious Moon used Kate to keep me in town long enough to get me writing his motherfucking book . . . and that you knew about it. Did he sabotage my car, too?"

Archer reached out his hand, but I moved for the exit.

"Talk to the girl," Archer said. "Talk to Kate!"

"Fuck you twice, Archer. And tell Moon to find some other goddamn sucker to write his piece of garbage!"

I slammed the door.

Part Four

I met Jack Williams at the university. He was an artist for art's sake. As such he was at the beck and call of art, although in Jack's case, art did not call that often. I did not envy him this schedule, although I admit there were times I would have welcomed such a luxury. For someone with such nonchalance, he managed to turn out pieces of impressive quality. Apparently, when art did call, it was a demanding mistress. He was a fantastic artist. His pieces had that layered complexity that made one feel a thousand things, paintings one could look at a thousand times and feel as if it were the first. His first big break was when he was twenty and a well-known art critic took him under her wing. She flew him east and presented him to the exclusive art world of New York. He received a commission worth one hundred thousand dollars, but failed to deliver on time, a mistake that delivered something of a black mark on his record

I would not say he was lazy. When he wanted to work there was not anyone in the world who could keep up with him. His favorite thing to do was simply nothing, interspersed with regular bouts of drinking and overeating fine foods. Such habits were hell on his meager bank account, not to mention his health, so he relied heavily on the good graces of the aforementioned critic, one of the few elite who had not abandoned him. Gloria Beckham, sixty, still clung to the idea that Jack was a genius and that one day he would be recognized and she would be hailed as his discoverer and benefactor. Jack was a genius; he simply did not have the same goals as Gloria. He had been careful to conceal this fact from her, although it was obvious to everyone else, but even the longsuffering Gloria had limits. I learned this one night over drinks, coming to the bar after a long day of pounding the keyboard to meet Jack, who had come to the bar after a long day of drinking. He was rarely down, but tonight looked completely depressed.

"It's started again," he said.

"Started?" I asked, waving to the waitress. She came over. She was all hips and cleavage and short skirt.

I could not keep my eyes off the waitress as she took my order of whiskey and onion rings. I glanced once at Jack to catch his eye, but he was staring into his old-fashioned. Then again, Jack had never shown much interest in any woman but Gloria.

"Gloria," he said, after the waitress had walked away. My eyes followed her.

"What about Gloria?"

"She's started again. She wants me to paint more."

"So paint more."

"I can't just paint more. You know that. It doesn't work like that for me."

"Did you tell her that?"

"She says she's through waiting. She says she'll stop with the money."

"She has said that before."

"I think she means it this time."

My drink arrived. "What makes you think so?"

"It's different this time," Jack said. "I know it."

I pushed his drink closer to him and, as the onion rings

arrived, nudged them his way. "It will be fine. Drink up, eat up, and maybe Mistress Art will pay you a visit in the morning. How many do you have so far?"

"Three."

"One better than last year and two months earlier."

"They're bad paintings. I forced them."

"Forced them?"

"Worked without the inspiration."

"You forced yourself to work?" Both the question and my attitude seemed sarcastic, but I was genuinely surprised and inexplicably unsettled. This was not the Jack Williams I knew.

"I know," he said. "Isn't it awful? They're bloody dreadful, too."

"Has Gloria seen them?"

"No, thank God. And she won't, unless she forces my hand. Which may happen if she goes through with this money thing."

"Then you should hope and pray you start painting good shit."

* * *

"So you have come to hear her read, have you?" Professor Schmidt sipped from a quarter full glass of scotch. Ice clinked against the beveled sides. He made a soft slurping sound as he drank. His white beard was well trimmed, not meticulous, and his white hair was brushed back, away from his face. It fell over his ears and was thin near the back. His nose, narrow at the top, rounded as it went and the end was pocked from early adulthood acne. His cheeks, what could be seen past the beard, were also marred, but the effect, surely unbecoming in his younger days, now combined with wrinkles to give him a wise, weathered look.

"I have known Chloe since college," I said. "I read her book before it was ever published."

"What did you think?"

"I liked it. A bit maudlin, perhaps."

"Poetry can be many things, but it should not be that."

"No. Have you read the book?"

"No."

"I am surprised she did not send you one of the advance copies."

"She may have." Schmidt wore a brown corduroy sports jacket, the kind that should have leather patches sewn onto the elbows, and a pair of dark wash jeans. He fingered a worn spot on the jacket's lapel. "She may have. I do not often review first work. I get enough of that in my classes." He slurped his drink. "I am somewhat surprised she beat you to publication. Based on your college coursework, I would have bet on you getting there first, especially given your work ethic. Still writing a thousand words daily?"

"At least."

"How many novels?"

"Five."

"None published?"

"Not yet."

"Prospects?"

"I have one on the market."

"Being shopped."

"Yes."

"I am surprised she beat you to it." Schmidt slurped. "She is a talented girl, but I fear her work may be doomed to failure."

"I heard you the first time."

"Calm down, calm down." Schmidt held up a pacifying hand. "It will come. I would have thought you would enjoy hearing how much I prefer your writing. Chloe writes as she lives. Maudlin, I believe you said. Ah, but here she comes now."

Chloe Parker wafted toward us on a breeze of success. It was her night and she looked it. Face aglow, body wrapped in red cloth that showed off her exquisite form, eyes shining, she was the picture of fulfillment. She was also as high as a kite.

"So glad you could come, darlings," she said dramatically, channeling her inner Tallulah. "Lovely turnout, isn't it?"

"Not bad for a poetry reading," I said. "Who else is joining you?"

"Joining me?"

"Yes. I understand this is a combined author event." I managed to take some of the glow out of her face.

"Oh, yes. Two other Chicago authors are reading."

"Who is sponsoring the event?"

"Our publishers, mostly, but the university arts council is giving us the building and music." She pointed toward a corner where some musicians sat, wearing evening dress and looking simultaneously smug and bewildered.

Schmidt grimaced as they began playing Stravinsky's *Three Pieces for String Quartet*. He regained control and said, "It must be quite a feeling of accomplishment. It is difficult to sell poetry these days."

"I'm lucky. My publisher is very supportive of the arts, not just commercial ventures."

"Do not sell yourself short," Schmidt said. "You were one of my most talented students. I feel as though I have a vested interest in making sure you are successful in your writing."

"No pressure, though," I said.

Schmidt released a little huff of air through his nostrils. "Success in the arts is not measured in money or fame. It is about reaching that inner sanctum where the purest form of artistry takes place. Like Hemingway said, it is about learning to write one true sentence. Once you do that, you have succeeded, even if you are living on the street and subsisting on cans of beans." Schmidt paused to slurp at his scotch, muttering something that sounded like an epithet against Stravinsky.

"Once a professor," Chloe said, smiling. "If you two will excuse me, I have to get ready for my reading. I'm up first."

We watched her walk away. It was hard not to.

"You sure changed your tune," I said. "The moment before she walked up her writing was mediocre and suddenly she is one of your most talented students."

"Do not be petty. Let her have her night. Tonight she will revel in her success. Tomorrow the literary world will tear her apart. She will lose that glow soon enough."

Chloe's reading was spectacular. Everything worked in her favor. The lighting, her clothes, the receptiveness of the audience, and, to some degree, her poetry, created a charged atmosphere that had listeners leaning forward to see her better, to hear her better, as if missing a detail or syllable would make a difference in their lives. Her voice carried well and for a moment I did not editorialize as she read, or think how I would have written it differently. When she was done, there was a moment of silence, as if the audience could not believe it was actually over, and then the applause was loud and long and sincere.

"You went over well," I said.

It was dark outside, but I could see Chloe's face shining. It had rained and the sidewalk and street were shining. The whole night was shining. Chloe was wearing a black and white, thigh-length coat against the October chill and her shoulders were squeezed up toward her chin. But she was smiling, happy, cheeks rosy and warm; it was my heart that felt cold.

"I think they liked me," she said, before throwing her arms wide and saying in a tearful voice, "You like me! Right now! You like me!"

"Okay, Sally, take it down a notch."

She dropped her arms and looked at me. "Oh, don't get stuffy. I'm just feeling good."

I pulled my own coat tighter and saw a taxi coming. Puddles dotted the street and reflected city lights. I watched the taxi as it broke through the puddles and they burst like fireworks in a spray of sparkling water droplets and it occurred to me, in a microsecond of surrealism, that the puddles were more beautiful when broken. Then the moment was gone and I was waving for the taxi.

"I could use a drink," I said. I got into the taxi and scooted to the far side.

Chloe hesitated, but followed.

"Nouveau Brasserie," I told the driver.

We rode in silence for a minute, pretending to watch the muted city nightlife, with its happy inhabitants, as it passed us by.

"We could have had a drink back there," Chloe said.

"I was tired of that place," I said. "They were stingy with the mixtures."

"My drink was good."

"Glad to hear it. We can get better ones at the Nouveau."

"I haven't been there in a while."

"It is difficult to go out if you refuse to answer my calls."

"You don't call."

"I have called. More than once."

"Maybe twice."

"And you decided not to answer either one."

"I answered one of them."

"That detail escapes me."

"You were drunk."

"Probably."

I leaned back in the seat and continued to watch the passing city. On the corner, two men stood close together and made a covert business deal. A quick slip of money and grab of a small bag. In the shadows of a store front, lovers writhed against one another. The night had grown darker, it seemed; the city certainly had.

"You didn't call," Chloe said, "except when you were drunk. And that is why we haven't gone out in a while."

"Sorry," I said.

"Why do you only call when you're drunk?"

"Maybe I am always drunk."

"You're not drunk now."

"I am not sober, either."

Chloe moved across the seat until her body just touched mine. "I wish you'd call."

"I will call. And besides, we are together now."

"I wish you were happy for me."

"I am happy for you." But I did not look at her.

She looked at me and then out the far window. "I miss you."

"I miss you, too."

Her hair was shining and I wanted to touch it, kiss it.

"I miss you so much."

"I will call."

She moved her hand to my arm and I reached up to touch her hair, feeling the softness, and then we kissed. It was a deep kiss and I was happy, happy for me and happy for her, and I wanted her book to sell a million copies.

"I miss you," I said.

She looked at me and smiled. "You meant it that time," she said.

The taxi stopped and we got out.

The Nouveau Brasserie was decidedly not new. It was over a hundred years old and showed each year in the wooden siding darkened with age and weather. But it was close to my apartment and the bartender served the drinks with the right amount of alcohol. I spent more time there than in my apartment and with the money I had spent I could have purchased a stake in the business. It was said Hemingway once drank there, but no one had ever been able to confirm the story. The assertion was mostly championed by the owner, who had reason for wanting the increased notoriety. The sketchiness of the claim did not discourage various literary types from frequenting the bar, in the hope of capturing any remaining shreds of genius Hemingway might have left floating around the place. I had spent many hours writing there, as it was cool and quiet during the day. Tonight the place was warm and loud, and not conducive to creation of any kind, except that of the bartender, who was busily making his own works of art.

I went to the bar to get drinks and as I waited, Jack walked in with a young man in frameless glasses and thinning hair that he wore combed straight back. Jack saw Chloe and went to her table. I got the drinks and joined them. Jack put a hand on my shoulder. He smelled like an old rag soaked in bourbon. His breath assaulted me. Revolted, I pushed his hand off my shoulder.

"Good God, is everyone high tonight but me?"

"And whose fault is that?"

"You seem in fine spirits," I said.

"Actually, I'm horribly depressed. The alcohol is helping."

"What is the occasion?"

"It's kind of a secret." Jack slurred the words so much I almost did not understand them. He began to giggle uncontrollably and his friend was forced to hold him upright.

"I love secrets," Chloe said. "Do tell."

Jack looked at her in wonder, as if he had not noticed her before. He grabbed her arm earnestly and turned to his friend. As he spoke, his voice rose higher and ended in a squeak. "John, meet the best fucking poet in Chicago, Chloe Parker. Her book was recently published."

John held out his hand. "Congratulations."

"Nice to meet you, John."

"And this," Jack said, looking at me, "is the biggest son of a bitch in Chicago. But a good friend and a damn fine writer, too."

I shook John's offered hand. "I hope you do not mind meeting the footnote," I said.

"Don't mind him," Jack said. "He gets a little sensitive when writing is involved. That's where the son of a bitch part comes in. If it weren't for his artistic sensibilities, he'd be a fine fellow. But then I suppose that goes for all artists, doesn't it?" He let out a peal of unattractive laughter and jumped to his feet. "I'll get drinks!" And then he was off toward the bar, running like a gazelle and shouting orders at the bartender.

"He's a little drunk," John said.

"We know," I said. "We are well acquainted with Jack. Sometimes it is better this way."

"Yes, but he doesn't paint much when drunk," John said.

"He doesn't paint much when sober," I said.

Jack returned shortly, his hands full of drinks. "Tequila shots for all!" He only spilled a little as he set down the shot glasses. He pushed one toward each of us. "What shall we drink to?"

"How about that big secret you won't share?" Chloe said. "But you'll have to tell us first. I think that's a rule."

"Is it?" Jack said.

Chloe and I nodded, and although the darkness of the bar made it difficult to tell for sure, it looked like John blushed.

"Ah, very well," Jack said, teetering, "but it must stay at this table."

I looked at Chloe, who smiled back and mouthed the words, "He's gay."

My mouth dropped open. Jack was gay?

"John and I are together." The words rushed out almost as one and Jack stood, heaving great breaths and looking back and forth at us, trying to gauge our reactions.

Chloe jumped up and hugged first Jack and then John. "That's so awesome, you guys! Congratulations!"

Jack beamed at her genuine praise. I mustered a small "good for you" and shook their hands. John's was soft and moist.

Chloe picked up her tequila shot and raised it over her head. "To Jack and John!"

And we drank.

* * *

The phone rang at 10:30 a.m. It was Jack. He was hungover and terrified.

"I had a dream last night," he said.

"Was it about being gay?"

"It was about telling you and Chloe that I'm gay."

"That was no dream."

"Shit."

"So it is true?"

Silence.

"It sounded true last night," I said.

"Yeah, it's true. John and I . . . we're a couple."

"You called just to confirm that I knew?"

"I want to know that you aren't going to tell anyone. I wouldn't have told anyone, either, except John has been pestering me to go public. I got a little too drunk and was in a good mood . . . you know how it is."

"Not really."

"Don't be an ass. The point is, if Gloria finds out about this,

I'm fucked."

"It sounds like you cannot avoid it."

"I hate you. Just promise me you'll keep your mouth shut."

I promised and hung up.

It was then I saw the phone message again, the one I had avoided all morning. I did not need to listen to the message to know what it said. It was the same every year. My mother became sentimental around the holidays and called to ask me to come for family Christmas. I would make up an excuse that did not fool either of us. She would ask about my writing in the way she had that let me know she and my father did not approve of how I was living my life, that I needed to find Jesus and get a real job. She would drop needling little remarks about how I might need the family someday and once she and my father were gone I would look back and wish I had spent more time with them. I would say I would think about Christmas. She would know I was not coming and would cry. I would hang up and know I was not going.

I continued avoiding the message as I sat down at my rickety desk and tried to make the words come. I worked for several hours and finished only two pages, not including the countless words I deleted as a result of false starts. As a typist, I was only fair, but even I could usually finish ten double-spaced pages during the course of a day's work. I pressed my finger on the "Backspace" key and held it down until the computer protested by beeping loudly.

I got up and listened to the message. It could have been a repeat of every message from every year, except this time she sounded a little saner. Perhaps the years of treatment and the occasional inpatient program were finally paying off. She also did not ask about my writing and ended by saying, "I really think you should come home for Christmas this year. Your father has cancer."

I stood there, still. My father had never paid much attention to his health, but this kind of call always came as a shock. At first

I felt a pang of pity and a tiny urge to go home, to be of some assistance. But then I remembered the years of judgment, the constant dismissal of my work, my mother in and out of facilities throughout my high school and college years . . . the bruises. The bruises. And then I knew my father could die a thousand deaths and I would not be there. I found myself hoping he would live long enough to watch me become successful in the field he so despised, long enough that I would be able to shower them with all the things they could not afford on their own, as if by doing so I would be able to show them how poor a life they had actually led.

* * *

The Nouveau Brasserie was quiet when I met Chloe and Jack for lunch. But then it usually was during the day. Chloe was there alone when I first arrived and it seemed to me she was a little colder than usual.

"How have you been?" she asked. Her arms were crossed. When men speak with their arms crossed, it is often nothing more than a sign of their own insecurity. When women speak with their arms crossed, it means they are pissed about something.

I sat down. "Busy."

"Writing?"

"Trying to."

The hard edges of her face softened, but she did not uncross her arms. "You'll get something, someone as talented as you."

There is something in the artist, the struggling artist, that revolts against the boundless confidence of others, even when it regards the artist's own work. Well-meaning people speak highly of the artist's efforts, but instead of being encouraging, it serves only as a reminder that the artist has, thus far, proven a failure. This was my internal reaction to Chloe's attempts to comfort me, the emotional equivalent of swatting away the hand that moves to pat one on the head. Even so, I knew what she intended and for some reason, perhaps the absence of alcohol, I was able to take it as such.

"It is my sixth novel."

"You should let me read the others."

"Why would you want to read five failed novels?"

"Maybe I can help."

"You write poetry." It came out harsher than intended and the lines of her face hardened again.

"I write other things. I have a collection of short fiction I'm shopping right now. My agent has it."

"And when were you going to tell me that?"

"You don't call."

"I have been busy."

"I know, writing. Maybe you write too much."

"It is what I do."

"Yes, I know. But maybe you should take some time to live."

"Writing is living to me."

"You can be very pretentious." She uncrossed her arms and reached out to touch my hand and I let her. "But I'm not complaining; so can I."

Jack slid onto a chair and John sat across from him. No one had mentioned John would be there.

"Hello, you two," Jack said. "Why so serious?"

"We're discussing how pretentious we are," Chloe said. She could turn on a smile like no one else.

"Excellent. Can we be pretentious with you?"

"Always," Chloe said. "Nice to see you again, John."

"John's here as moral support," Jack said.

"Moral support for what?" I asked.

"I've been painting like fuck for the last couple of weeks and

I'm sending what I've done, along with the others from earlier in the year, for showing consideration at Prentiss."

"The independent art gallery?"

"The same."

I looked at Jack with unconvinced interest. This was an abrupt about face for him, going from an artist wallowing in self-pity to one with the confidence to submit a collection to the philanthropic, but selective, Prentiss gallery. I looked at John, who was smiling proudly, and back to Jack, who looked misty-eyed and even hopeful.

"I thought you did not like what you had created so far this year. I believe 'bloody dreadful' were the words you used."

"I may have overstated my loathing for them. As you will recall, I was drunk when I said that."

"I would lay odds on you being drunk right now."

"Yes, but I have my head on straight."

"Why the sudden change?"

"Oh, lay off him," Chloe said. The note of disgust in her voice pricked me. "You're like a terrier. I think it's fantastic Jack wants to show at Prentiss and I have no doubt he'll be accepted."

"You think so?" Jack said.

"Absolutely! What's the deadline?"

"Proposals have to be in by mid-November. The winner will be chosen in early January and the show takes place in February."

"Quick timeline," I said. "Do you think you will be ready?"

"For fuck's sake." Chloe wanted to hit me. I could see it, already feel it. "Let the man revel a little in his newly discovered ambition, will you?"

"He'll be ready," John said. He punched Jack lightly on the arm. "If he isn't, he'll have me to contend with. I can be pretty violent."

The discrepancy between the good natured threat and John's

petite size made Chloe laugh, which made me like John a little less.

"So tell me, John," Chloe said, "what do you do when you're not helping struggling artists?"

"Being a struggling artist," John said.

"Oh no, not another one," Chloe said. "You poor thing. Not a writer, I hope." She glanced daggers at me.

"An actor, actually. Theater. Although I do write a little on the side."

I cringed and felt a twinge of dread in my stomach. People who wrote on the side were usually also people who thought about writing a book on a weekend, as if it were the easiest thing in the world, like frying an egg or walking to the gas station for beer. Jack saw the look on my face and interpreted it correctly, as I knew he had the same reservations about come-lately artists.

"He's talented," he said, poking a thumb at John. "I was surprised when I first read his work."

The feeling in my stomach tightened. "Why do I feel this is leading up to something?"

"Jack told me about you," John said. "He says you are quite good."

"And?"

"And I was hoping you would look at some work of mine and give me an idea of how I'm doing. You know, structurally."

"Jack did tell you that I am unpublished, right?"

"He said you just hadn't found the right publisher."

"Or the right manuscript," I said, wincing.

"I know you're probably swamped with your own work," John said, "but I was hoping you'd have some time to look at mine." He reached inside his jacket and pulled out a compact disc. He put it on the table and nudged it toward me.

"I am not sure I—"

"Oh, come on," Chloe said. "It would do you good to get your mind off your own writing. Maybe this is just what you need to refocus."

"There's no hurry," John said. "Just take the disc and if you get to it, then great. If not, I'll understand."

I did not want to take the disc. If I did, it would hang over my head for weeks and I had enough to worry about with my own writing and Christmas and cancer. And what if I read it and it was as awful as I expected? Or, even worse, what if it was good? I looked around the table and they were all looking at me and in the end it was easier to take the disc than explain why I could not.

"I have no idea when I will get to it," I said. "It could be some time."

"No problem," John said. "I have time. I just want to get better. I have immense respect for the craft of writing. I know it doesn't come easily. I would appreciate any help or advice you could give me."

"I will see what I can do," I said.

Both Jack and John excused themselves soon after, a move that caused me to suspect their motivation for coming at all had been to drop off the manuscript. I turned to Chloe to say as much, but she was smiling at me as if I had rescued a puppy from a mountain lion.

"That was a very selfless thing to do," she said. "I know how much you hate reading manuscripts from novice writers."

"If you knew, you would not be so happy about it."

"Well, anyway, I'm proud of you."

"Fuck you."

"We haven't done that in a while."

Her words were electric and I wanted her. "My apartment is close by."

"Finish your drink," she said.

* * *

I did not finish the drink, but we finished together and lay back on the bed in helpless post-coitus, breathing hard and wondering why we had waited so long.

"I'm worried about my book," she said, once she had recovered enough to speak in full sentences. "The reviews."

"What about them?"

"My publisher is expecting reviews from some established New York critics."

"And you are worried they will be bad?"

"They could ruin the book. I'm counting on positive critical reception to cement my reputation with the publisher. We know that poetry isn't generally a commercial success, but they are hoping to get the attention of academia. If my collection is panned, the publisher won't take a chance on being embarrassed a second time. I'll be out."

"I think you are overreacting."

"I don't think so. It has happened to others."

"You will be fine."

We lay there, naked, feeling the cool breeze coming through the open window.

Chloe asked, "Do you think I'm a good writer?"

"I heard you read at the book launch."

"Yes, but do you think I'm good enough?"

"You should not be worrying about that right now. You need to stay focused. You should be proud of your success. You got published; that is more than I can say."

"You'll get there," Chloe said, moving close to me and resting her head on my shoulder. "I know you will."

I wanted to tell her how I really felt, how it did not seem right she should be published while other writers worked their asses to the bone without result. That it was not fair poets and mediocre writers could find publishers while other writers stacked failed novel on top of failed novel high enough to serve as a coffee table. I wanted to tell her my dad had cancer and that I did not care.

* * *

The holidays were upon us. Already stores were full of faux Christmas cheer: wreaths, garland, wrapping paper, holiday music being piped through tinny speakers. I tried to avoid this as much as possible, although it was impossible to block out completely. Even the Nouveau Brasserie succumbed to the pressure and set up a little Christmas tree at the far end of the bar with little twinkling, colored lights that ran through a preprogrammed list of routines every five minutes. I found it maddening and had to sit with my back to the tree to keep from taking it out into the alley and stomping until it blinked its final blink.

I mentioned this to Professor Schmidt one day when he joined me for a pint. He observed the tree with a watery eye, as if weighing its artistic merits for a class discussion.

"I agree it is quite awful," he said. "Although I suspect not the source of your general malaise. Writing issues?"

"You know me too well."

"I know writing too well."

"It is not going swimmingly, I will admit."

"What seems to be the problem?"

"If I knew that—"

"You know it," said Schmidt, sliding comfortably into the role of professor, a persona he never entirely shed. "You simply have to allow yourself to see it."

"I really do not know. It just will not come."

"I seem to remember you having similar trouble with other

manuscripts."

"This is different. Every other time I had a certain confidence it would eventually come. This one is different."

"How different?"

"I do not have that confidence."

"So it is simply an issue of confidence."

"I suppose. But there is something else. Something that makes me feel the lack of confidence is not unfounded."

"You are tired," Schmidt said, "that is all."

"Maybe if I stopped wasting my time with frivolous dreams and did something realistic, like law school or something in the sciences."

Schmidt grimaced. "Disgusting. I still have confidence in you. The mere fact I am sitting here drinking with you should illustrate that. I do not maintain relationships with most of my students, as most of them are complete washouts, unimaginative dolts who would be much better off going to law school or some other such peasantry. But you . . . you have something. I thought so from the moment you turned in your first assignment. It was rough work, yes, but there was something in your voice, an innate understanding of literature and structure. That is why I have stayed in touch, with you and Chloe. You both exhibited that unique tone. I have never been proven wrong on this."

"Her reading went well."

"Indeed it did. I am proud of her, although I do worry somewhat about what the future holds."

"Why do you say that?"

"The world is not often kind to poets. Besides, I am not sure the critics are ready for her work."

"What makes you think it will not fare well?"

"It is different than the kind of thing that is popular now," Schmidt said. "Her publisher may have done her a disservice by agreeing to release the collection."

"She can always write other things. I remember her writing some short stories back in school."

Schmidt shook his head vehemently. "No, her genius is poetry, not prose."

"But if it would be better received—"

"The world owes the artist nothing. The artist owes the world everything. Chloe's talent is one which may not be recognized until long after her death and, although her apparent failure now may seem tragic, it is simply the way of things."

"That seems harsh."

"Only if we view ourselves with an inflated sense of importance. We artists are nothing; it is the art. We are only conduits. When the artist becomes the art, the art itself dies."

"Was that intended to cheer me up? Because now I need another drink."

Schmidt pushed back from the table. The chair legs scraped on the floor. "You will have to drink alone. I have a meeting at the college that, while it promises to be obscenely dull, I really should attend." He stood and paused, his hands clasped as if in prayer. "You should send your work-in-progress to me. I would be willing to take a look and see if I can stick a pin in exactly what the problem may be."

"Chloe offered the same thing."

"Then perhaps you should take her up on it. The life of an artist is hard enough. Why insist on making it more difficult than it has to be? Take help when it is offered. You never know when it might come around again."

Although I was sure his words were not intended to sound sinister, they had that effect. I watched him pay his tab and stride from the bar, shoulders slightly slumped, one hand tucked into his jacket pocket, the other swinging freely. I watched him, and wondered if perhaps teaching writing, instead of actually doing it, might not show the man's real wisdom. When I had been a student in his class, and thoroughly in awe of his command of literature, I had searched high and low for something he had published, but come up empty. Any direct inquiries were met with either deflection or glib remarks about how it was some people's calling to write and others to teach. But he knew too well the psyche and struggles of the writer. I watched him, and wondered what he wrote about when he was alone with his words.

* * *

It was at the end of a long night of writing that I remembered John's disc. I had written an entire chapter, but when I reread the words, they were horrible and forced, dry and meaningless. At least I could read something assuredly more awful. I felt inside my jacket; the disc was still there. I inserted it into my laptop with more force than necessary. The man was not even a writer, he was an actor, and now he had the audacity to think he could sit down and turn out a novel. It might feel nice to read the rough, unpracticed prose of someone who had no business writing in the first place. The file opened and pages of text scrolled before my eyes.

Before I was ten pages in, I badly needed a shot. I had been determined to dislike the work, convinced I would have little trouble doing so, but to my utter horror I discovered the book was good. More than good. It was the kind of work I had been struggling to complete. The prose was liquid fire, but simple and sweet and raw. The characters jumped from the page and spoke like real people and moved through the story with ease. John had somehow managed to smooth the novel's rough portions while maintaining a beautiful raggedness that made it breathe. Little tweaks of the text, though not revolutionary, made it so real that it seemed to tremble on the screen. The only thing I wanted was to have written this story.

All that week I seethed about John's book and how it so diminished my own writing efforts. It could not be as good as I thought. It was impossible. In desperation, I e-mailed the file to Professor Schmidt, taking care to remove John's name from the manuscript. I did not know how well Schmidt knew John, if at all, and did not want to risk word getting back to John that I had sent his book to someone else. Perhaps Schmidt would read it with a clearer perspective and be able to point out any fatal flaws it may have.

I received a phone message from Schmidt, inviting me to his upcoming holiday party. It came as a relief, an explanation I could give my mother. I told her it was an important networking opportunity, an excuse that turned out to be true.

Schmidt's seasonal parties were well known among the literati and artistic circles. In order to receive an invitation, one had to achieve a certain status among Schmidt's cadre, one defined by the man himself. Chloe had published something recently, which I supposed made her of more interest, but I could not deny the sting that came from being an apparent last minute choice.

"I'm sure it was just a simple oversight," Chloe said when I complained to her. "I'm lucky the party is happening before the reviews come out, after which I will likely be anathema to the Chicago literary scene."

"At least you are getting reviews."

"How long are you going to pout about that? Stop being such a child."

"'When I was a child, I spoke as a child, I understood as a child,

I thought as a child: but when I became a man, I put away childish things.'"

"Shakespeare?"

"The Apostle Paul. First Corinthians 13:11."

"You remembered that from your childhood?"

"There are some things you do not forget."

* * *

I arrived at Professor Schmidt's large old house feeling self-conscious in my rented dinner jacket. The sleeves were short, which caused me to constantly tug them down, as if I could stretch the fabric just a bit. Schmidt himself answered the door and his face brightened as he saw me. He grabbed me in a hug I was too surprised to evade. He had clearly been drinking, but something else was up. I feared I knew what it was.

"My dear boy. Let me look at you." He released me from the hug and grasped my shoulders, holding me at arm's length and grinning like a furry Carroll creation. He inspected me with beaming pride, as if looking over a piece of artwork he had just completed. "My boy, you have done it. You have really done it. I knew it was only a matter of time. From the moment I first read your work in my class, I said to myself, 'Schmidt, you can mold this boy into something great.' And I have been proven correct."

I wriggled in his grasp and he dropped his hands, but lost none of his ebullience. I had trouble meeting his adoring gaze. "What are you talking about?"

He deliberately tilted back his head and laughed loudly, attracting not a little attention. "Playing coy, are we? The manuscript, you little wanker! The manuscript!"

"You liked it, then."

"Liked—liked it? No, no, I did not *like* it. I *prize* it. I devoured it from beginning to end in a single evening, a single sitting. As you know, I rarely do that with any author's work."

I had not, in fact, known this, and found the knowledge unsettling. "So happy you enjoyed it. About the manuscript—" And then I realized I would not be able to tell him. I would not be able to break the spell of his adoration. As uncomfortable as it made me and as shitty as I was beginning to feel, I knew I would not be able to tell the truth. I told myself it would be cruel to disappoint Schmidt, who had clearly decided to take a generous portion of credit for himself. But I knew it was really because I loved the feeling of admiration and respect. It was what I had been working for and now that I had it, even if through means not of my own making, it hit me like a drug.

"Come along," Schmidt said, putting his arm around me. "I have some people I want you to meet. Maxwell!" He waved at a tall man standing by the hors d'oeuvres. The man walked over and I recognized him by his picture from an article in *The Paris Review*. He was Pete Maxwell, an influential editor credited with discovering several prominent names in contemporary literature.

Maxwell walked toward us. His gait was wide and swinging, like a cowboy just off the range.

"Maxwell, I want you to meet the next big thing in literary fiction." He turned to me. "This is Pete Maxwell. You might have heard of him."

I nodded and took Maxwell's offered hand. "I read your article in *The Paris Review*. It is a pleasure to meet you."

"And it sounds like I should be happy to meet you," Maxwell said. His voice had a decided Texas drawl, not at all what I would have expected from a high profile editor. He looked at Schmidt. "Your offspring?"

"Christ, no!" Schmidt looked so horrified I felt a little hurt. "I do not have children."

"That you know of," Maxwell said. He gave me a sly wink. "So tell me, why should I be excited about you?"

My mind froze as I tried to think of a way to sell another writer's work, but Schmidt jumped in before I even had to try.

"This young fellow sent me his latest novel and, I speak honestly, I could not stop reading the damn thing. Read it from beginning to end, in one sitting."

Maxwell looked impressed. "You never do that."

"Precisely," Schmidt said. "The boy has something."

The editor looked me over as intently as Schmidt had, although with a good deal more calculation. "Well, I've never known Schmidt to be too far wrong on these things," he said. "I'll introduce you to a few folks and we can talk. Then I'll have to read this masterpiece of yours, of course, but if it's as good as the old goat says, then perhaps we can work something out."

The rest of the evening was a blur of quick introductions. Within the first hour I had a pocketful of business cards that would have otherwise taken me twenty years to collect. The party was a writhing nest of literary powers, with a few minor players thrown in, and I began to get a sense of how high the odds were stacked against outsiders. Nepotism reigned supreme and without a connection or the proper introduction, one could despair of striking the deal every writer dreams of. I thought about Chloe and her family's money and wondered if that was how she had gotten her publishing contract. Looking around the room I wondered, if this was how it was in every publishing circle, how any new voices could ever be heard. Of course there were publishing options, and indie publishing was on the rise, but there still remained the problems of reputation and distribution. The sheer economics of it all was enough to make my head spin and I knew the opportunity staring me in the face would not come around again.

Thinking of Chloe reminded me I had not seen her all evening. During a break in the action, I asked Schmidt if he had seen her.

"Chloe? No, I think not."

"She told me you had invited her."

"Well, I had."

"You speak in past tense."

"In light of recent events I thought it best to rescind the invitation."

"You disinvited Chloe?"

"I did." Schmidt held a cocktail from which he calmly slurped. He spoke of rescinding the invitation as casually as someone else might mention having sushi for lunch. "I thought it best. Poor girl."

"Poor girl?" I tugged at the sleeves of my jacket.

"You have not heard, then?"

"Heard what?"

"The reviews came in for her book."

"And?"

"Devastating. Completely devastating. She is finished, I would say."

"They could not have been that bad."

"They were worse. I told you her publisher might have done her a disservice by publishing her work. It simply was not time."

"But why disinvite her?"

"Look around you." Schmidt gestured with his cocktail glass. "This is the best attended gala in literature. And by that I do not mean it has the most attendees. My parties are legendary in the literary world because of who attends. People do not just come to eat miniature sandwiches and drink my expensive wine. This is where the magic happens. Book deals worth millions have been struck at these parties, professional alliances lasting twenty years have been forged here. I have to protect the reputation of my little gathering in order to meet the high expectations. Having Chloe here, in the aftermath of such brutal treatment by the critics, would have, I am afraid, cast a pall over the evening."

I looked at Schmidt, aghast at what I was hearing.

He smiled. "You looked shocked. And I cannot say I blame you. It can seem harsh if you do not fully understand how the system works."

"The system?"

Schmidt shook his head, as if bemoaning my naiveté. "It breaks my heart to crush your idealism, but everything has a system. As I recall, I mentioned to you how the world owes the artist nothing, that the artist is the one who owes the world."

"You did," I said, "but I thought you were speaking of the responsibility of art."

"That is exactly what I was speaking of. Art has a responsibility to put itself out there to be enjoyed, judged, used, and consumed. And in order for that to happen, there must be a vehicle. There must be a mechanism in place to take art to the world."

"But all of these people," I gestured around the room, "and you, for that matter, are choosing what the world will and will not see."

"Someone must," Schmidt said. "Why not us? Who could possibly be better prepared than we to be the gatekeepers? Had Chloe's publisher been one of us, the poor girl would have been spared a good deal of embarrassment and would not have put her literary future in jeopardy." He slurped and raised an eyebrow. "You look a bit sickly."

"I feel a lot sickly."

"You will get over it. And I would advise you to do so quickly, as the night is young and your own future is being made as we speak. Think carefully."

I want to leave, I thought. *I should leave. I should tell Schmidt the manuscript is not mine and then just walk out the door and never come back*. I should get into a taxi and drive directly to Chloe's place and make love to her and tell her I am sorry. She will ask what for and I will say it does not matter. It will be wonderful and we will start a life together, away from this madness to which I have just been introduced. Perhaps I will get a real job, working with Chloe's father or a little shop downtown, and life will go on peacefully as I punch the clock, secure in my own principles.

But in the end I stayed. I stayed late into the night, drank both scotch and Schmidt's gushing compliments, surrendered to the lurid appeal of the entire scene. It was, after all, what I had always wanted, what I had worked for, what I had defied my parents and upbringing to achieve. And for the moment, as I drank my way from introduction to introduction, I was able to forget I had not gotten there on my own.

* * *

I stood in the darkness outside my apartment door and turned the key in the lock. Something hard hit my face and for a moment I lost all sensation. Then I felt the slow trickle of something wet. I reached up and found a cut on my forehead oozing blood. Instinctively I pushed open the door and stumbled inside. I groped for the light and noticed with bizarre indifference I left bloody fingerprints around the switch. I looked at the redness on my hand, curiously unafraid.

Jack followed me into the apartment. His fists were clenched, his face a mottled array of color and emotions: red and angry and purple and confused and white and hurt. He raised a fist to hit me again and I knew why he wanted to and I wanted him to, wanted him to hit me again and again. He was trying to hit me, I could tell, but he could not do it with the lights on.

"You motherfucker," he said. His voice was low and a little shaky. "What the hell is wrong with you? Didn't you think someone would know?"

"How did you find out?" I asked.

"Chloe heard from someone at the party she got disinvited from that you had finally written something readable and she asked Schmidt for a copy. He sent over a sample. She read it and knew it was good and asked me if I'd seen it. I said I hadn't and she sent me the same section. I've read John's book, man."

"Does John know?"

"I haven't told him. For some reason I thought maybe you would have an explanation. But the longer I waited, the angrier I got. If you have an explanation, now would be a good time to tell me, because I really want to kill you."

I had no explanation, so instead of answering, I shut the apartment door and walked to the kitchen where I grabbed a paper towel and held it to my head.

"Look, Jack, I am really sorry about this."

"Sorry? You can't just be sorry. You have to tell Schmidt."

"I cannot tell Schmidt."

"Actually, you can. And you will."

"I have worked hard, Jack." And as I said this, it made sense. Jack looked at me, his eyes wide. "It's not your manuscript!"

I opened the refrigerator and took out a beer. "Do you want a drink?"

"I'm serious, man," Jack said. "I will fucking kill you."

I knew I was being a shit, but somehow I felt a surge of self-righteous indignation. I turned to meet his gaze, making my eyes as cold and steely as I could. I was shocked by how good it felt.

"You are not going to do anything," I said.

"You don't think we can prove it belongs to John?"

I opened the beer and took a swallow. "No, I do not. How would you? The time stamp on a Word document? And who do you think Schmidt would believe? And besides, I do not think either you or John will risk having your relationship made public."

Jack's face drained of all color. "You asshole."

I forced myself to hold his stare.

"Who are you?" Jack said. It was a rhetorical question, spoken with conviction. "I thought we were friends."

"We are friends. I just . . . I need this."

"This isn't your manuscript!"

I could not look at him any longer. I was cold inside and I drank the beer in silence.

"Talk to me," Jack said. "What am I missing here? There has to be some way to fix this. You can write your own stuff; you've been doing it for years."

"Exactly."

"Do you want me to ask John if he would help you with some of your manuscripts? I'm sure he would."

"Get out, Jack."

It was not pretty, but finally he left and I knew I would not see him again. I expected to feel something—sadness, perhaps—but instead I just felt empty. I knew the right thing, of course, and it was not too late to do it. I could just call Schmidt, tell him there had been a mistake, forget all about it. Schmidt would be furious and embarrassed, but I was sure Jack would move on quickly enough and John did not yet know. That was when I thought of Chloe. Jack said Chloe had sent him the portion of manuscript.

My mouth dry, I called her number and waited. It rang and then it stopped ringing and there was silence. I could tell someone was on the other end, because I heard ambient noises.

"Chloe?"

There was more silence and I just waited. I heard a sniff and then,

"How could you?"

"Chloe, let me explain."

"No! There's nothing to explain. Just tell me if it's true or not."

"Chloe—"

"Tell me!"

"Okay, fine, it is true, but—"

"How could you do that to me?"

"To you?"

At first she would not speak and then I did not think she would stop.

"Yes, to me! I've stood behind you. You don't think it's been hard, supporting your dream, watching the world go by, while you shut yourself in your little cocoon, closing me out most of the time? All the while defending you against the people who were convinced we were both wasting our time? I've never said this to you before, but there aren't many people in this city who believe you have what it takes. I didn't want to hurt you; I knew you didn't need the distraction or the pressure. But Jack and I . . . we never lost faith in you. I waited for you. How could you do this? Can't you see what a betrayal this is?"

"It is not like that."

"Of course it is! I know you think you live in a vacuum, but you don't! Your actions actually do affect other people. You need to call Schmidt and tell him you made a mistake. Tell him anything."

"I cannot do that."

"Yes, you can."

"It is too late."

"You just don't want to. I see that now. I was hoping you just weren't thinking clearly, that it was all some big misunderstanding, but you're actually going to do this, aren't you? You want this so badly you're willing to do whatever it takes to get it."

"I need this." A pleading tone crept into my voice. "I am an artist, and I need this."

"Oh, please! You're not an artist. An artist creates, even imitates, but doesn't steal. You're no artist and you'll never be one. You once said you wanted to do something people would remember you for. Well, if that's what you wanted, I think you've succeeded. I just didn't think you would go this far to get it."

"Chl—"

She hung up and I held the silent phone to my ear.

* * *

I did not leave my apartment for days, except to walk to the convenience store for beer and a little food. I had no one to see. I had effectively alienated my social circle. It had been small before, and I knew I had not been the most communicative friend in the best of times, but knowing those connections were no longer an option caused a feeling of extreme isolation. In addition, I still struggled with my own conscience and was in no way as comfortable with my actions as my pride dictated I pretend. My thoughts turned more toward my own family and my father's cancer. I even had the fleeting thought of traveling home, but quickly dismissed this idea as the desperate ruminations of a madman. The last thing I needed was to go home and have my decisions questioned even further. Of course I knew I was doing something morally and artistically wrong. I even knew no amount of reasoning would justify it to anyone. Regardless of what Chloe and Jack might think, I had not somehow immunized myself against any knowledge of wrongdoing. And this knowledge weighed on me more than I wanted to admit.

The isolation grew worse by the day as my phone did not ring and my pride would not allow me to call anyone else first. When it finally did ring, it was Professor Schmidt and he wanted to meet me that evening at Gray's, a fashionable restaurant in a part of town much nicer than where I lived. Maxwell would be there. I was told to wear a jacket and be on time. My heart clenched as I wondered at the occasion. Had they discovered my secret? Or maybe Jack had decided to tell Schmidt the truth and risk that I might tell Gloria what was going on with John. I doubted I would go through with my own threat, but was gambling Jack would not take the chance. A worse thought was Chloe had decided to sell me out. That seemed to be a more likely scenario. She had been hurt and angry enough to do it, and had the scruples to back it up. Whether I was on the verge of being discovered or not, I was beginning to think the crushing weight of guilt and stress simply was not worth it and by the time evening came I had tentatively decided to confess everything. It would not take long. Just meet with Schmidt and Maxwell, tell them the awful truth, and leave. I would lose their support, but might be able to repair my relationships with Jack and Chloe.

I put on the only jacket I had, a black sport coat with a torn lining. I took a cab to Gray's and arrived five minutes early. I checked in with the maître d' and was led to a corner table illuminated by tasteful mood lighting, a darkened atmosphere I hoped would conceal the subpar quality of my jacket. Both Schmidt and Maxwell were enjoying an apéritif. Schmidt was dressed not much better than I, except his worn jacket had likely cost much more. Maxwell, dressed impeccably in a charcoal three piece suit, stood when I walked up and reached out to shake my hand. My hands were clammy, but I shook hands and sat down, wiping my palms on my pants.

"Brandy?" Schmidt asked, raising his glass.

"No, thank you," I said. I was wondering how I was going to

afford the meal itself and did not need to inflate the cost with tiny, overpriced liquors.

"Don't worry about the cost," Maxwell said. "This is on me."

This lightened my mood considerably, not just because it was welcome news to my bank account, but because it was not likely Maxwell would buy dinner for a plagiarist.

"Well, okay then," I said. My smile felt wobbly and must have looked pathetic, because both men chuckled. "Maybe one."

"Oh, there will be plenty of time for drinking," Schmidt said. "And plenty of cause, as well."

"Indeed?"

"Indeed." Maxwell finished off his apéritif and placed his hands palm down on the table as if bracing himself against an impact. He leaned forward and said, "I've read the manuscript."

The pronouncement was delivered with such gravity that, had it been a line from a DeMille biblical epic, would have been immediately followed by a crash of thunder. I tensed inside, as I always did when someone was about to make a pronouncement about my writing. And I thought vaguely how strange it seemed I was beginning to think of John's book as mine, even to the point of truly caring what people thought of it. Of course, it could have something to do with the fact it was being credited to me and, therefore, whether I had actually written it or not, it was my reputation as a writer at stake. A little voice in my head har-rumphed at the idea of my having any regard for my reputation as a writer. But through recent practice I had become adept at ignoring that little voice. And I did so now, with a bit of help from the waiter, who had just delivered my apéritif.

"And what did you think?"

"It's fucking marvelous," Maxwell said.

"You liked it, then." I glanced at Schmidt, who looked smug. My decision to come clean, tenuous at best, wavered, and I was disgusted by my susceptibility when it came to anyone praising my writing, or even what they thought was my writing.

Maxwell laughed a Texas laugh, entirely unsuited for this type of establishment. "I like anything I think will make me a good amount of money and this, my boy, will. I can sell the shit out of it."

"That is good to hear."

"You do not seem overly enthralled," Schmidt said.

"Sorry, it has been a long week."

"Completely understandable," Maxwell said. "I could have gotten back with you sooner, but I wanted to take my time with the manuscript. I've made a few notes I think might make it a little better, just even things up a bit, but the core story is excellent. It's really a fantastic piece."

"Thank you." I did not know what else to say, although it felt as if there should be more.

"We're going to make some money on this," Maxwell said. "I've been in the game for a long time now and I can feel it when I'm on to something. And this is something. I really do believe in your book." He reached inside his suit jacket and removed an envelope. "To that end, I want to offer you this. It's just an advance, mind you, and we'll certainly work out the royalty details, but it should give you some idea of how I feel about your fine book." He pushed the envelope across the table. I took it, held it.

"Well, open it up," Schmidt said.

I did so with shaking fingers.

"Fifty thousand dollars?" My voice cracked.

"As I said, it's just an advance," Maxwell said. "But that's still a good number for a book in this genre. If I didn't see something special in it, I wouldn't take the chance. But I want this book. We can do well together."

I stared at the check. I closed my eyes and then opened them again. The number was still there and burned into my eyes as if printed in fire. My weak resolve dissipated like steam off a teapot. Fifty thousand dollars was a lot of money. And Maxwell seemed to think it was only the beginning. My mind raced and I was only dimly aware of Maxwell continuing to talk, saying something about book clubs and national awards and a movie deal. And I saw it more clearly than ever before. This book was my ticket out of a marginal existence and into the light of legitimate authorship. No more wondering if I would have enough money each month to pay the rent on a shitty studio apartment overlooking a parking lot, no more scraping just to buy food and decent beer, no more struggling to write through continuous uncertainty. And, best of all, no more doubts from my own family. Furthermore, if I got to the top with this book, I would then have a market for my own work. Yes, it would have been preferable to make it completely on my own, but everyone needed a little help. There was an old business motto, "Fake it until you make it." Is that not what I was doing? I knew I was a good writer; I just needed to get someone's attention and then I would be set. I might get there on John's work, but I would stay there with my own. I would be a fool to turn this opportunity down. If I made enough, I could give money to Jack and John, in a sense paying for the use of John's manuscript. It would be like a loan. John would not know what to do with the book anyway. He did not have the experience or drive to use the platform as Maxwell was clearly planning. And this book would need to be succeeded by another and another. John might have been lucky with this manuscript, but he would not be able to follow it up with others like it. The opportunity would be wasted in his hands.

"I don't want to be unclear," Maxwell said, becoming more serious. "This money buys me the right to handle your book. I want you to know that before you take it. And, of course, you'll have to sign a provisional contract saying as much."

He produced another piece of paper. He slid it across the table and I read it over. If I signed the contract I would be locked in. There would be no going back. I looked at the check, and then back at the contract.

Schmidt seemed to sense my hesitancy. "You will never get a chance like this again. I know it is difficult to sign away your work, like giving up a child. From what I hear, that is difficult, heaven knows why. But this will change your life. For the better. Do not be a fool."

I would later try to remember how I felt at this time, as my eyes moved back and forth between the contract and the check. It was the presence of all feeling: happiness, fear, guilt, defiance, anger, vindication—all perfectly legitimate feelings, each beautiful in its own way. But together they were ugly, like mixing every color on an artist's palette to create a dirty brown hue.

I swallowed hard. "I am so sorry," I said, "but I am afraid I need to borrow a pen."

* * *

At a booksigning in Chicago, a young woman walked up to me. She had shoulder-length blonde hair and the greenest eyes I had seen in years.

"Emily?" I sat behind the signing table, unable to move. I realized my mouth was hanging open and I snapped it shut.

"Yeah, it's me." She looked around at the prominent display featuring my book and the line of readers behind her waiting for an autograph. "You've done well for yourself."

"Here today, gone tomorrow," I said. "How are you?"

"I'm good," she said, smiling and nodding with too much enthusiasm.

"My god, it has been years. What are you doing with yourself?"

A stocky guy in a Scooby t-shirt leaned out of line. "Hey, what's the hold up?"

I ignored him and said to Emily, "Can you stick around? I would love to catch up."

She did and we did. Over coffee we talked for hours and it was as if we had never been away. She was still the girl who taught me how to swim and I recalled the day with a smile.

"I was such a naughty thing," she said. "What you must have thought."

"I did not know what to think. It was the single best thing that had ever happened to me."

"Aw, how cute."

"I was not exactly a worldly fellow back in those days. My parents kept a tight leash on me."

"I remember."

"Needless to say, I broke out of there as soon as I could get a job to support myself."

"Do you keep in touch with them?"

"My father is not at all thrilled with my chosen field."

"Writing?"

"Naturally, he wanted me to do something within the church world."

"Writing isn't godly enough?"

"Not the stuff I write. And he views artistic pursuit as little more than a hobby anyway. When he finally accepted I was not going to follow in his pastoral footsteps, he pushed for business school. I think he figured I could at least make good money so I could support a church financially. They still have not given up on the idea that I will come around and rejoin the flock, although they are less intrusive than usual."

"Softening up?"

"Distracted. My father has cancer. He will not live out the year."

"I'm so sorry."

"I think he will be happy to be free of me. I have managed to disappoint him on every score."

"Still the resident atheist?"

"I really do not think about it anymore."

"That's funny."

"Why is that funny?"

"Well, I guess because I've thought about it quite a bit over the years."

"My atheism?"

"No, my own unbelief." She started playing with a ring on her right hand, twisting it around and around. I noticed her necklace, which was a crucifix hanging from a thin gold chain.

"You? You became religious?"

"I accepted Christ as my savior. I suppose that makes me religious."

For the second time that evening I was stunned. "I am shocked. I never would have guessed that the free-spirited girl I knew from all those summers ago would get religion. Wait . . . is that why you tracked me down?"

She laughed. "No. And I didn't track you down. I just saw the advertisements for your book event and thought I'd come see you."

"I am glad you did."

"Me, too."

I leaned back in my chair. "Are you too religious to go for a real drink?"

"Hell, no," she said. "Let's get out of here."

We drank more than one drink and she came back to my hotel. I lay on my back with her sitting naked atop me, the gold cross swinging between her breasts. It was perfect, as if this was always meant to happen. Easy, natural, and we came almost simultaneously. Afterward, we lay under sheets and stared at the ceiling. I realized I was smiling and when I looked over, she was smiling, too.

"I don't want to be without you," she said.

"I do not want you to be without me."

"We should stay together."

"Yes."

It all happened so fast. Looking back, I could see the folly of it all. But I wanted it, could not be without it. It was as if the past had shown up to remedy the present. And it made me forget how I had gotten there. We dated furiously for a few weeks and then got married. The royalties from the book allowed us to honeymoon in style. For two weeks we cruised the Caribbean, hired help plying us with drinks. We baked in the golden sun, soaked up green-blue water. The never ending party helped me ignore the warning signs of Emily's instability, an unsettled quality she had not possessed when we were kids. The days flew by and then we were back in the Midwest. It was January.

Emily grew quieter and more distant as time went by. The restless, agitated girl from the honeymoon changed to one moody and increasingly withdrawn. I could not seem to reach her. Her interest in sex diminished soon after the honeymoon and six months into our marriage, we stopped fucking altogether. She began to let her appearance go, not just venturing outdoors without makeup, but neglecting to wash her hair and not bothering to match her clothing. She began wandering around the apartment naked, which at first excited me, but then became strange. She was turning into a zombie, devoid of emotion. That warm, sensual creature who had whispered "we should stay together" was a thing of the past. I knew it had to be me. I was a disappointment to her, was letting her down. At the same time, I deeply resented her refusal to tell me how I could improve the relationship.

One night, I lay awake. Sex was foremost on my mind and I seethed at what had become consistent rejection. Somehow I decided pushing the issue would be a good idea, as if she just needed to be reminded how much she missed it. She snored lightly. I moved my hand under the covers and cupped her left breast. She rolled away and mumbled something unintelligible. I moved onto my side and drew closer until the contours of my body matched hers. She stirred and I traced the outline of her ear with my lips. My hardness pushed against her and she must have felt it, because she came awake with a start. She pulled back, a look of revulsion on her face.

"What are you doing?" Her eyes looked at me, but did not seem to actually see my face.

"I . . . I just thought . . ."

"I'm not your whore! I'm not your sex slave!" She slid from the bed, stumbled on a pile of old laundry, then stood there, shaking. The gold crucifix hung from her neck, impotent. "What the fuck!"

"Em?"

"Don't call me that! Don't ever fucking call me that!"

"Emily, it is just me."

"Stop coming into my room! I'm going to tell mom!"

I tried to talk to her the next day, but she refused to look at me, much less carry on a conversation. She packed a small bag and left in a cab. I looked through the things she had left behind and found a few pills hidden in random places. A background check revealed several drug-related charges. Now I understood that the girl on honeymoon had been a girl recently off drugs; the girl in marriage had been a girl back on them. It was not much of a comfort, since I should have been able to guess what was happening. Or maybe I had known and had not wanted to confront it. I spent as much time and money as I could muster looking for her. The police were of limited help, so I hired a private investigator whose search turned up little.

"She's traveling light and likely using cash," he said. "That usually means she's also traveling fast. Nobody seems to remember seeing anyone like the girl I describe, so it's possible she's changed her appearance. I can keep looking, but I have to tell you it's probably a waste of time. If she was anywhere around here, I would have turned up something by now. I guess you'll have to ask yourself how much you want to find someone who wants to stay hidden this bad."

I paid the investigator's fee and let him go.

I began hanging around the bookstore where she had made her appearance, even after my book stopped selling so well and people stopped recognizing me. I knew, along with my agent and Maxwell, it was time to write another book, but I could not seem to catch the muse. I do not know why I spent so much time at that bookstore; I did not really believe Emily would reappear. And if she did, what then? Would we really get back together and live happily ever after? Our marriage had been insane, as if we had thought we could recapture the innocence from a summer long ago. She had a recurring drug problem and was obviously fighting some manner of mental disturbance over something in her past. I remembered what she had said all those summers ago in Serenity after being grounded for shoplifting.

"My dad goes a little nuts. I didn't think I'd ever get out of my room," she had said. "Or him, either."

During the final meltdown before her disappearance, she had threatened to "tell mom." That could not have been directed at me. It was obvious now that Frank Dunbar was an even bigger sleazebag than I had thought. His early abuse probably had a lot to do with Emily's current drug problem and general instability, which in turn made it impossible to deal with any PTSD resulting from the abuse. It seemed I had spent too much of my life hating a man I did not even know. And yet, somehow, I felt I knew him all too well.

* * *

It would be a stretch to say I got over Emily. But eventually I did resume writing, partly under pressure from Maxwell and partly because I knew the only way to write was simply to do it. Just as Emily had forced me to let go of the pier after I thought I was going to drown, and just as people thrown from horses must get right back on one, I had to begin writing again. Interest in the first book had waned and I worked feverishly to turn out something equal in craft and similar in interest. Weeks went by during which I kept insane, unrelenting hours. Ninety thousand words later I began revising. And then it was off to my agent. After reading the manuscript, she was tepid in her praise, but forwarded it to Maxwell anyway. It was published early the following year.

Sales were disappointing, not just because it had been too long between releases, but because the new book was not up to its predecessor's quality. The critics' reactions varied from lukewarm to frosty, including one superfluously savage review from the *Chicago Times*, written by the same reviewer who not that long ago had bemoaned the fact of having but two thumbs to turn upward in favor of my previous book—John's book.

The new book moved quickly from feature to bargain and my agent informed me bookstores had been forced to return an unseemly number of copies to the publisher. I did not have to be told that meant my relationship with that particular publisher had come to an end. Midlist writers cannot afford to flop and I had just flopped. Maxwell and Schmidt stopped returning my calls and I sat alone at my laptop, writing, because it was all I knew how to do.

The loneliness was crushing, while the thought of having others around became even worse. I began drinking more and sleeping less, as fitful dreams and sweat-inducing nightmares often filled my nights. I began seeing things: visions or hallucinations. They were minor at first, a fleeting shadow on the wall or a sound I could not identify. Then I saw other things: a stream of blood under the door, a figure standing in the corner. I would blink and the image would disappear. I chalked it up to drink and exhaustion, and kept writing—trying to—living on the few royalties from John's book. A Hollywood studio bought the rights for a reasonable sum and it became a book club selection the year after. It is always surprising, however, how much money it actually takes to maintain a decent existence in the United States and it was not long before my bank account was dangerously low. I wrote puff pieces for magazines and journals, and managed to make ends meet, but time spent writing crap was time not spent on my comeback novel. Even though writing magazine articles was not the same as novel writing, it still ate up a lot of time and creative energy. But bills had to be paid, so I wrote about smart shopping techniques, the best foods for a robust sex life, the top ten places to raise a family, anything to bring in a quick payday.

My daily existence became a rhythm of ritual and because I existed on such a razor's edge, I came to loathe any change to the system, anything that might throw my fragile world into chaos. I went grocery shopping at the same time because I learned when the store expected new deliveries, which meant they often had sales a day or two before in order to make room for new inventory. I went to my favorite coffee shop on Tuesdays because my drink of choice—the chai tea latte—was beverage of the day. Over time, everything found its place. I ate the same things on the same days, I brushed my teeth with the same toothpaste and in the same way, I went to bed and got up at the same times, I placed my slippers in exactly the same position every night, I always slept on the same side of the bed, I arranged the cans in the pantry by food, size, and color of label. All these things and more took over my life. Only through strict order was I able to maintain a level of control, a sense of stability, even if it was but an illusion.

There are, no doubt, many people of ritual. I would venture to say everyone has a level of routine. They like certain things at certain times. It is, indeed, comforting. Yet I began to obsess about my rituals, playing directly into the tendencies I had displayed since childhood. As they infiltrated my life, I became increasingly agitated when things happened to disrupt what I had come to view as the natural order of my life. One incident involved my regular order of Chinese delivery that arrived ten minutes past its scheduled time. Infuriated, I called the manager. I was a regular customer and one who, over time, had spent a good deal of money at that restaurant. I do not recall exactly what I said, but at some point I must have demanded the firing of the delivery boy, because he never delivered another item to me. I saw him later, as he bagged my groceries and refused to make eye contact.

Through the domination of my habitual living, I still held onto the dream of writing a comeback novel, even though my obligation to writing anything saleable made it nearly impossible to turn out quality fiction. I began to associate my lack of production with my location and became convinced a new locale would work wonders. I began living more frugally and threw myself into writing commercial pieces. Before long I had enough to fund a small trip to the Upper Peninsula.

That first trip hooked me. I rented a small, rustic cabin for a week and wrote like a man possessed. I drove home with a stack of manuscript pages heavy enough to hold a door open. A few months later I repeated the trip with the same result. Not everything I wrote during these excursions was publishable, of course, or even decent. But that did not matter. I was writing. Soon I was convinced I would only be able to write—really write—during these northern excursions. It was like setting forth on a voyage to meet the writing god who showed me the way. The north was my mountain and I was Muhammed.

PART FIVE

I stepped from the shower and wiped the steam from the mirror to continue my morning ritual. Shave, hair, teeth. White t-shirt, dress pants and shirt, tie, jacket, shoes. By then the steam had completely faded and I looked at my reflection. A regular joe, a suit and tie on the way to an office to make sure a room full of cubicle-bound cretins did not screw up a client's invoices. Being a business manager was, quite possibly, the worst job I could have. But then again, not many places were hiring a forty-ish man with no previous work experience.

I left my apartment at precisely 7:41 a.m. and parked my car at 7:58. That gave me just enough time to jog into the building and slip into my office. A good manager would be there to welcome their employees. I was not a good manager. I was the deadbeat dad of managers, the one who took long lunch breaks and fell asleep at his desk and left dirty coffee mugs in the kitchen sink.

"Excuse me, sir?"

I looked up to see Carol Grifkin poking her shrewish head into my office. Her protruding teeth always looked like they should be busy grinding the impregnable shell of a walnut.

"What is it, Carol?"

"I'm going to have to leave early today. My little boy is sick and the sitter can only stay until noon. Is that okay?"

"You have a child?"

"Yes, sir. I'm married, of course."

"How reassuring," I said. I left her standing there and started a game of computer solitaire.

"So . . . can I take the half day, sir?"

"Fine." I did not look up.

She scuttled away. I felt a nap coming on.

My cell phone rang. It was a number I did not recognize and at first I was going to let voicemail pick it up. But then I realized I had nothing better to do. I hoped it was a telemarketer. They were the only ones with jobs worse than mine. I supposed coal mining might be worse. At least with coal mining there was a chance you would die young. I answered the phone.

"Hello?"

"This is Clayton Marsdale. I'm an attorney in Lansing, Michigan. I represent Mr. Nigel Moon. May I confirm to whom I am speaking?"

I told him.

"As you may have heard, sir, Mr. Moon passed away a little while back. As his attorney, I'm tasked with managing the estate."

"No, I had not heard about his death," I said. "How did he die?"

"He drowned. He was in the Upper Peninsula at the time. He suffered from dementia and we can only assume he became confused, wandered into the water and went too far out. There were a couple of witnesses who saw it happen, but they were too far away to help by the time they realized what was happening. They said he just walked straight into the waves until they went over his head. The tide was strong that day and by the time help arrived he was gone."

"What does this all have to do with me?"

"The rights to his name are yours. Everything else went to his only granddaughter. He was very clear about his name, that you should have the rights. I've spoken with his publisher. You should expect a call from her to discuss how you both want to proceed. In the meantime, I'll send you all the necessary paperwork."

"Thank you for letting me know," I said.

"I'm sorry for your loss. You two must have been close."

"Not really."

But perhaps we had been closer than I realized. I sat back in my chair, overcome with a complete and unexpected sense of loss. I had not known Moon that well, not really, and we had not parted on the best of terms. But now that he was gone, I felt something had been stolen from me. Not innocence, exactly, but a sense of possibility, of hope. I wondered if he had ever found someone to write the book I had started. I had not heard anything about a new release, so I assumed it had simply died along with our friendship.

I pulled open the top desk drawer. There was a book inside. I took it and thumbed the worn pages, reading wherever my eyes landed.

"There is a time," the book said, "when each man is faced with the test of his existence. Everything he has experienced to that point has molded him, honed him, groomed him for that moment. How he faces that test—whether with solid grace or capricious temper—will determine how the rest of his life will proceed."

Those were Moon's words, written so many years earlier in *The Lonely Peninsula*. I had read them many times before and each time they struck a note within me, but even more now that he was forever gone from my life. I had not thought I would see him again, but the possibility always existed. Now even that had disappeared. And I was not sure if it made me happy or sad. I was left with a curious feeling of quiet stillness, almost reverence, as if any movement or noise would be sacrilege.

I do not know how long I sat there, but eventually I stood up. I picked up my workbag and walked from the office, down the hall, and out into the sunlight. I went to my car and drove away. I did not speak to anyone or even look back.

* * *

"Welcome to Pine Lake," the clerk said. He looked at me over tiny, square glasses. "What you say your name was?"

I pointed to my driver's license that lay facing him on the countertop.

"Oh, right," he said. "Didn't see it. Eyesight's not what it used to be, although I never was much for spottin' things. Wore glasses since I were eight year old. Wearin' glasses is tough on a kid, you know, especially when you're just wantin' to run and play with the rest of the chil'ren." He was mostly bald on top and what few strands remained he wore long and slicked back, where they congregated with the hair on the back of his head to complete a greasy ponytail. He was unshaven, with a week's growth on his face and neck. As he spoke I could see he had not invested in a good dental plan over the years. He peered at my license. "Okay, Mr.—what's that say? Oh, yes." He typed something into his ancient computer and squinted at the screen. "Looks like you're in Cabin 5." He handed me a key. "You know the way?"

"I will be fine."

"I could show you the way. We're not too busy, ya know. It ain't peak season. Once July hits, watch out!"

"I will be fine."

"Used to be nothin' here, of course, 'cept an old fishin' pier. But once they set up this little retreat and changed the name of the lake, people started flockin' in. You sure you don't want me to walk you over?"

"No."

"Okay, if you're sure. Watch out for the squirrels! They love gettin' fed and can be a wee bit aggressive."

I left the office with as much speed as my heavy duffel bag would allow.

Cabin 5 was not far. I put the key in the lock. It turned easily enough and I walked inside. It smelled of dust and stale air, which I remedied by opening a window. I unzipped my duffel and pulled out a gray case. I opened it, revealing a 1952 Underwood typewriter recently purchased on eBay. I set it on the table and spooled in a piece of paper. I centered the type guide and placed my hands in position over the keys. They slowly lowered to feel the cool, metallic key faces. A breeze came through the window, rustling the single page. A bird sang. A wave lapped against a rock or tree root. A bee hummed past the window. I started humming, and surprised myself with the tune as I began to mutter the words.

What can wash away my sins?
Nothing but the blood of Jesus—

I stopped singing, expecting to be thrown into some insane hallucination.

Nothing.

The bee returned, passing the window again, its hum reassuring.

I felt the breeze; it both cooled and warmed me. I caught the musty aroma of impending summer. It was a spiritual moment, one I had missed for years, that moment before beginning a new work. It was like raising a child or what I imagined raising a child would be like. What would I call it? How would it grow? Would I love it, like it, hate it? Would it mind me or would I mind it? Would it mature quickly or take its time? How would it interact with its peers? Would others like it or find it spoiled and overly precocious?

I sighed, took a deep breath, closed my eyes. My fingers pressed the keys. I watched the black marks as they pounded into life against the page. They were, in fact, living things, wrenched violently into existence as if through birth. *Bang, bang, bang.* The letters appeared slowly. There was no particular hurry. I stopped typing and looked at what I had written. It was not much, but it represented much.

"*The Peninsula, Revisited,*" the page said. "By Nigel Moon."

Enjoy the book?
We'd love to have a review
on Amazon.com!

ABOUT THE AUTHOR

Craig A. Hart is the stay-at-home father of twin boys, a writer, editor, Amazon bestselling author, lover of the arts, and only human.

He has served as editor-in-chief of the *Rusty Nail* literary magazine, manager of Sweatshoppe Media, and director of Northern Illinois Radio Information Service. He lives and writes in northern Illinois with his wife, sons, and two cats.

Visit him on Twitter and Facebook, or by visiting his website at www.craigahart.com.

Made in the USA
San Bernardino, CA
11 November 2015